RACING
THE MOON

RACING THE MOON

MICHELLE MORGAN

ALLEN&UNWIN
SYDNEY • MELBOURNE • AUCKLAND • LONDON

First published in 2014

Copyright © Michelle Morgan, 2014

Allen & Unwin
83 Alexander Street
Crows Nest NSW 2065
Australia
Phone: (61 2) 8425 0100
Email: info@allenandunwin.com
Web: www.allenandunwin.com

A Cataloguing-in-Publication entry is available from the National Library
of Australia
www.trove.nla.gov.au

ISBN 978 1 74331 635 1

p. viii-xi: Sydney Harbour Bridge photography by Sam Hood courtesy of the
State Library of NSW – DGON4/782

Teachers' notes available from www.allenandunwin.com

Design and illustration by Astred Hicks/Design Cherry
Set in Baskerville 12/20pt by Peter Guo/LetterSpaced
This book was printed in May 2014 by Griffin Press,
168 Cross Keys Road, Salisbury South SA 5106

10 9 8 7 6 5 4 3   14 15 16 17 18 19

With love to my family ...

CONTENTS

EGGS

What a year! Don Bradman scored 334 runs in the Third Test against England, the half-arches of the Sydney Harbour Bridge finally met in the middle, Phar Lap won the Melbourne Cup, and Harry and I went into the egg business together. Harry's been my best friend for as long as I can remember. We catch the train every Friday after school to Uncle George's chook farm to pick up two boxes of eggs – that's twenty dozen or 240 eggs. We get them at cost price for a shilling a dozen and sell them for two shillings. Not bad for a couple of Glebe boys on the wrong side of thirteen. There are no overheads – even the train fare's free. We're not breaking the law because there's never anyone to collect our tickets at Rooty Hill station.

Harry and I have food rationing to thank for our thriving business. Eggs are as scarce as hen's teeth. You line up for hours with your food voucher and by the time you get to the top of the line, there are none left. Good old Uncle George!

'Selling eggs shouldn't be a crime,' Dad says, 'and if you don't get caught, it won't be.'

Dad really knows his stuff. He bought and sold Uncle George's eggs until his illegal bookmaking business started taking off. It might be the Depression, but there are plenty of opportunities to make money. The world is my oyster! Dad hasn't looked back and neither will I. Friends, neighbours and total strangers come to our house at 51 Abbey Road every Saturday morning to buy 'Joe and Harry's Extra Large Farm Fresh Eggs'. That's what we painted on the back fence. And 'Home deliveries free of charge'. You've got to have the edge over your competitors to stay ahead of the game.

Climbing the side fence into Old Billy McCarthy's yard to deliver his usual dozen eggs, I heard someone screech, 'Shameful, just shameful!' The voice was human but bird-like, a cross between a kookaburra and a cockatoo. Old Billy stopped pruning the hydrangeas with his rusty shears. I looked around, half-expecting to find a strangled chook hanging upside down from Old Billy's clothes line, but instead saw Miss Ruxton peering over her front fence. She's a scary old lady who moved across the road a couple of months ago.

'Who are all those men coming and going like dogs on heat through the Rileys' back fence? I've been watching them every Saturday since I moved here. It's shameful, just shameful!' she called out to Old Billy. Miss Ruxton's glasses magnified her brown eyes, making them look really big and too close together.

I tried to look invisible, but I was stuck between a rock and a hard place.

'Good morning, Sybil,' Old Billy replied. 'What a glorious day! You're looking very beautiful.'

What's wrong with that man's eyesight? I thought. I nearly choked trying not to laugh, then I started coughing and couldn't stop. The eggs were bumping together inside the newspaper parcel, so I quickly handed them to Old Billy. My face was burning and my eyes felt like they were ready to pop.

Miss Ruxton was pointing at my house. 'I know what goes on in there. I wasn't born yesterday!' She smoothed back her feathery wisps of grey hair to reveal cheeks almost as crimson as the lipstick that was smudged around her beak-like mouth.

'You've got the wrong end of the stick, my dear,' Old Billy replied, patting me on the back to help ease the coughing. 'The Rileys are a good Catholic family, except for Arthur, of course, he's Church of England. Young Joe here's an altar boy.' Old Billy pointed his rusty shears at me, nearly poking me in the eye, and then put them down to unwrap the eggs. 'Look at these beauties! Joe sells eggs for his Uncle George. Has a farm out west somewhere. Why don't you order some? Guaranteed double-yolkers in every dozen!'

Miss Ruxton crossed the road, looking at me with

those piercing eyes, sizing me up. 'Eggs? All those men come through your back fence to buy eggs? What's that wireless for, then? It blasts away all day, every Saturday. Eggs, you say? You can't fool me.'

I didn't know what to say, then Old Billy came to the rescue. 'I'm not sure what you're getting at, my dear. Arthur and Betty are keen as mustard on the races and they've got the best and clearest wireless in Abbey Road.'

'Tell me about it!' Miss Ruxton opened Old Billy's gate, staring at me the whole time. I started walking backwards but I couldn't get away from those eyes.

'Stand still, boy, I'm not going to bite, I just want to look at you. Tell me the truth. Do all those men come to your place every Saturday to buy eggs and listen to the horse races on your wireless?'

I nodded. 'Yes, Miss Ruxton.' True, of course, but only half the story.

'You'll have to excuse me, Sybil. I have to pay a boy for some eggs,' Old Billy said, tipping his hat – he's a true gentleman. Reaching into the pocket of his overalls, he then handed me two shiny new shillings.

I rubbed them together. Cash in my hand always gives me confidence.

'Let me know when you want some eggs, Miss Ruxton,' I said. 'Special delivery for the prettiest lady in the street!' Old Billy winked at me before going inside.

'You're quite a salesman, young man. Put me down for half a dozen. No broken ones, mind.'

'You bet! I'll deliver them to you free of charge every Saturday morning. Total cost, one shilling.' *Another happy customer,* I thought as I watched her cross the road back to her house. *But I'd better stop throwing stones on her roof – bad for business.*

I'm saving up to buy Mum a cottage by the sea. She's been talking about it for as long as I can remember. She wants to hear the ocean roar and look out her kitchen window to see the waves rolling in, just like she used to. Mum grew up in a fishing village on the south coast, and hasn't been back since she ran away with Dad sixteen years ago.

The wireless blaring isn't the only noise coming from our house. There's lots of shouting and arguing most days. Old Billy used to break up the arguments between Mum and Dad until last year when I took over the job. I'm nearly as tall as Dad, and not nearly as scared of him as I used to be. I'm the second tallest boy in my school but not for too much longer. I'm off to high school in a few weeks.

RACE DAY
CHAPTER 2

Saturday is race day – it starts like any other day then the tension starts to build. There's important work to be done, and the sooner we get breakfast and chores out of the way, the better.

This Saturday you could have cut the tension in our place with a knife. Dad got home late the night before and Mum was giving him the silent treatment. It was the Anniversary Day long weekend with races on Saturday and Monday at Randwick Racecourse to celebrate the landing of Captain Arthur Phillip and the First Fleet on 26 January 1788. Dad was going to be flat out all weekend. The big races – the Anniversary Handicap and the Adrian Knox Stakes – were on Monday with big prize money for the winners. The Adrian Knox Stakes is a race for three-year-old fillies only, which is rare in horseracing.

'It gives the fillies a chance to race without having to worry about the colts getting too frisky and excited,' Dad explained.

Dad knows all about getting frisky and excited, I caught him in the act once. Mum was still in hospital with Matilda. I heard voices upstairs and thought they'd come home early. I ran into the bedroom then stopped dead in my tracks. There was Dad in bed with another woman. I don't think he saw me; he was way too busy. I ran away as fast as I could. Dad called out but I didn't answer. He must have figured out it was me; he's been out to get me ever since.

That morning, my little brother Kit and I were eating breakfast quickly, crunching and munching loudly, trying to outdo each other. I grabbed a third piece of buttered toast, demolishing it while Kit was still on his second. We slurped hot, sweet, milky tea in between mouthfuls.

Dad threw his cup into the sink, smashing it. 'I've had enough of this! I work seven days a week, and this is the thanks I get?' He glared at Mum and she glared at him.

'I can smell it on you,' she said.

'Can you smell it now?' Dad lifted Mum off her chair with one hand. 'Don't you ever speak to me like that!' he said.

I jumped up, grabbing his hand as he went to slap her across the face.

He pushed me hard against the wall. 'You stay out of this! It's between me and your mother.' He grabbed Mum by the arm. 'It's my business what I do on a Friday night. Now come on, we've got work to do.'

Mum squeezed my hand on the way past. It was her way of telling me that she was alright.

While Dad was going to be busy taking bets for the Anniversary Day races, I was planning to be four blocks away with Harry, taking bets for the Glebe Derby, the biggest billycart race in Sydney.

Dad had locked my old billycart in the back shed to punish me for almost burning the house down, when all I was trying to do was light a really hot fire to unblock the chimney in the lounge room. I'd already tried using the poker but the soot wouldn't budge. Old Billy told me that lighting a hot fire is a cheaper and better way to unblock a chimney than hiring a chimneysweep. I was keen to put it to the test.

The wood was a bit damp and I couldn't get the fire started, so I splashed on some petrol, chucked on screwed-up newspaper and threw a match in. It all burst into flames but instead of burning through the soot, it filled the room with smoke. I could hardly breathe. Just when I was about to give up and put out the fire, the flames started racing up the chimney like wildfire. Everything went quiet for a couple of seconds before the thunder. I thought the chimney was going to explode. I ran outside just in time to see black smoke and feathers shooting out all over the roof then raced back in to inspect the damage before Dad did. The smell of burnt pigeon and starling combined with the petrol fumes was really disgusting. Soot, feathers and small charred bodies were all over the lounge room. It was much worse than when I'd tried to push Kit down the chimney to prove there was no Father Christmas.

I didn't burn the house down but I did unblock the chimney – clean as a whistle! Then it took me all day to clean up the mess inside and out. I got the usual belting and to top it off, Dad locked up my old billycart, just because I'd brought it into the house. I had to bring the wood and petrol inside somehow. That old thing was falling apart anyway. I was going to throw it on the fire if the petrol didn't work but it worked a treat.

What Dad didn't realise was that my old billycart had already been replaced by a newer model. Harry and I built the best billycart ever at his nan's house. I was the Glebe Billycart Derby champion, and was defending my title at three o'clock, the same time as the fourth race at Randwick. My regular Saturday chores would have to wait because I had bigger fish to fry.

THE DERBY

Harry and I couldn't take the bets fast enough. There was a big turnout for the race, bigger than we'd expected. Not just kids but adults as well, and they all wanted a piece of the action. While Kit was busy marking out the starting positions on the road with chalk, I checked out the competition.

I was up against five other billycarts – three locals and two blow-ins. Sid Dunn was my only real threat, he'd been trying to beat me for the past two years, and came close last year. Sid's cousin, Stan, was racing Sid's old billycart, and the other blow-in was that new kid from Cowra. Only been in Glebe a week and thought he could win the Derby. No chance! Gordon always comes last in his fruit box on wheels. I didn't expect it'd be any different this year – same Gordon, same fruit box. Tommy Fisher didn't have a hope in hell. He was only ten, the same age as Kit, and way too young to handle the pressure of a big race like this.

Being the Glebe Billycart Derby champion, I was the favourite to win. Judging by the bets being placed, most of the punters thought so too. Harry and I did some quick calculations and worked out that we'd be at least thirty shillings in front if I lost the race. Kit was beside himself.

'What do you mean "lose the race"? You're going to win, aren't you?' Kit asked, picking his nose. He does that when he gets nervous or upset.

'We're running a business here, not a charity. The whole point of the Derby is to make money.' I tried to give him a brotherly hug but he pushed me away.

'You're the Glebe Derby champion – don't you

care about that?' It was touching that Kit was more concerned about my reputation than the money we'd be making.

'Of course I do, but only when I've got better odds. I'll win the Derby next time or maybe the time after that. It all depends.'

'I don't get it. How can we win money if you lose the race?'

'Haven't ya parents taught ya nothin'?' Harry almost spat at Kit, rolling his eyes in disgust. 'We make bucket loads of cash if Joe loses 'cos we don't hafta pay the punters nothin'.'

Kit still wasn't happy. 'Why did we go to so much trouble building a new billycart if you're only going to lose? Why did you take the wheels off Matilda's pram?' He was shaking and looked like he was about to cry.

My mind was focused on billycarts, not family heirlooms. I had a race to lose. I climbed into the billycart, shifting my body about to get a feel for the new model. I looked at Sid, my main competition, and stared him down.

Harry was ready with the starter's gun. 'On ya marks, get set—'

When the gun sounded, I was off. The billycarts rolled together down the road, getting ready for the big downhill section. At the top of the hill, I could see people lined up on both sides of the road, cheering for their favourites. I accelerated down the hill, faster than I'd ever gone before. *Must be Matilda's pram wheels*, I thought. I flew over bumps and potholes, and took the bend in the road with ease. I was a nose in front of my nearest rival and we were well in front of the others, damn it! This called for desperate measures. I pulled on my rope and steered across the road, ramming the new kid from Cowra.

'Piss off!' he shouted. He managed to pull free but we were drawn together again like magnets, and our wheels locked.

'Get off me!' he screamed.

'I can't!' I screamed back.

We skidded for several yards, still locked firmly together and about to win the race. I tugged on my rope as hard as I could. We both swerved, crashing into a garbage bin that was lying in the gutter and then spun into a lamppost, the force of which finally threw us apart, not far from the finish line but not close enough, thank God! Sid Dunn won, his cousin Stan came second, Tommy came third, and Gordon came last for the third year in a row, a new race record. The new kid from Cowra and I were disqualified for going outside the race boundaries.

Harry paid five shillings to each of the two punters who'd bet on the winner, and then started counting all the money that was left − our winnings. Gordon, who had come last in the race, was quietly watching Harry. Standing next to him was a tall, thin man wearing an old hat that was pulled down over his eyes.

'I know what ya did and me son wants 'is money back,' the man said.

'I dunno what ya talkin' 'bout,' Harry replied.

'I heard ya talkin' before 'bout throwin' the race. Ya said ya'd make more money that way.'

'Well ya heard wrong, mister. Sid Dunn won fair 'n' square.'

'Give me son 'is money back!'

'Piss off!' Harry replied, staring the man down.

'Ya haven't heard the last of this. Gordon, go get ya billycart, we're goin' home.'

I may have lost the race and the respect of a few people, but Harry and I won thirty-six shillings. I also got much more than I bargained for. As I picked myself up from the gutter, my right arm went limp and started to throb. 'Bugger it!' I yelled at the peeling paint on the lamppost.

'Ya bloody idiot! Ya didn't hafta crash it. That's four weeks' work down the drain,' Harry said, kicking the broken pieces of billycart off the road. 'Here's ya share o' the winnin's.' He dropped eighteen shillings into my hand. 'Don't forget the cricket match tomorra. I'll pick ya up at eight.' He headed back up the hill whistling. Harry's not the most sympathetic bloke, but he's still my best mate.

'You could've won the Derby easily if you wanted to,' Kit said, picking up the four pram wheels from the gutter, inspecting each of them. Surprisingly, they looked as good as new.

'Here's a couple of bob for helping me out with the

race,' I said, trying to give Kit two shiny new shillings. 'Ow!' I screamed, clutching my sore arm.

'I don't want your money,' he said, walking away. He went a few yards up the road and then stopped. 'How's your arm?' he called out.

'Bloody sore – I think I've broken it.'

'I'm going to put the wheels back on Matilda's pram before Mum notices they're gone. Are you coming?'

'You bet!' I might have scored a broken arm but I had a pocketful of money and was feeling almost on top of the world. Kit wasn't so happy – he didn't say another word to me the rest of the way home.

BROKEN ARM
CHAPTER 4

After sneaking through the back gate, Kit went into the shed to put the wheels back on Matilda's pram, while I crept along the outside wall of the house. I looked in the window and saw Noni, my big sister, dancing around the kitchen, holding a dress in front of her. When I tapped on the glass, she screamed. I pointed upstairs to where I hoped Mum and Dad were still working. Noni waved for me to come in.

'Where have you been? The washing is still on

the clothesline and if you don't split some wood for the stove, we won't be able to boil the kettle, let alone cook dinner,' she said, huffing and puffing like the little red engine.

'I think I've broken my arm again. It's the right one this time,' I said, sounding sorry for myself. I was in a lot of pain and all I could think about was how I was going to explain my broken arm to Mum and Dad when I was supposed to be at home all afternoon doing chores.

'Dad'll kill you when he finds out, and it'll serve you right!' Noni said, staring at me like she was searching for the truth.

She can stare as long as she likes, I thought, *she's wasting her time.*

'What lies are you going to tell this time?' She was almost shouting. I was lucky that the wireless was blaring away upstairs with one of the races at Randwick or Dad would've heard everything. I'm not sure if it was the throbbing in my arm or the thought of another belting from Dad, but I felt very light-headed.

When I came to, I was sitting on a chair with Noni slapping my face. 'Stop that!' I said, trying to grab her hand. 'Ow!' I'd forgotten about my broken arm.

'Sit up straight and stop whingeing. Let me think,' she said, pacing up and down the kitchen. For a fifteen-year-old girl who's five foot nothing, she can be very intimidating.

'I'll lie for you, if you lie for me. I'll say that you were helping me hang the new curtains in the kitchen when you fell off the sink and broke your arm.'

Hardly a challenge, I thought. 'What's my lie?' I asked, almost keen. Lying was my forté.

'You'll owe me one.'

'Fair enough,' I replied, quite impressed with Noni's effort. Kit came into the kitchen, carrying an armful of wood and dumped it on the hearth in front of the fuel stove. 'Thanks mate,' I said. 'How did you go with the wheels?'

'Good as new.'

When Dad came downstairs, I told my lie convincingly about how I'd fallen off the sink and broken my arm. It went better than I'd thought it would.

'Accidents happen,' he said. 'Noni, you'd better take Joe to the hospital while your mother and I listen to the last race and then do the books.'

He was in an unusually good mood, particularly after the bad start we'd had that morning. I even detected a small skip in his step.

'It's been one of our best days ever. I hope the favourites keep up their losing streak on Monday. I'd better get back to it – the last race is about to start,' he said, getting a bottle of beer out of the ice chest. He went back upstairs, whistling.

Noni wasn't at all happy about having to take me to the hospital. She poked me in the chest and said: 'You owe me double!' She glared at me as she put on her hat and then headed for the front door. 'Are you coming to the hospital or not?'

It was after eight o'clock when we got back. My arm was in plaster and I was really hungry – I hadn't eaten anything since breakfast. Mum was busy sewing and Dad was sitting in his armchair, looking like the cat that ate the canary.

'Hey Betty, the hospital won't need to keep so much plaster on hand anymore,' he said, winking at Mum.

I had no idea what he was talking about so I laughed just in case I should. It was more of a grimace really. I was in pain, and Dad was no comedian.

'How did you manage to fall off the sink?' Mum asked, looking up from her sewing.

'It was wet from the washing up. I slipped and lost my balance,' I replied, trying not to make eye contact.

She took off her glasses and looked into my soul the way she always does. That's who Noni gets it from. I almost blurted out the truth but then I saw the warning glimmer of Dad's belt buckle and thought better of it; I was in no fit state for a belting.

'Your dinner's on the stove. Noni, would you mind serving it up while I finish this buttonhole?' Mum asked, putting her glasses back on.

ALTAR BOYS

I tossed and turned all night, waking up to the sound of *tick, tock, tick, tock, tick*. I opened my eyes and looked across at the clock. 'Shit!' Jumping out of bed, I kicked off my pyjama pants and pulled my shirt over my head, ripping off all the buttons. I hopped about trying to get my shorts on, and then got the plaster on my arm stuck in the sleeve of my best shirt. I ran down the stairs, two at a time, my shirt flapping behind me.

'Mum!' I called out.

She was at the stove cooking scrambled eggs. 'It's alright, Kit's filling in for you.'

'He can't do that! He's not even a proper altar boy; I'm still training him.'

Mum helped me put my shirt on properly and then did up the buttons. 'You can sit back for a change and enjoy Mass with the rest of us.'

Dad says it's one of life's little mysteries that I'm an altar boy. With a name like Joseph Francis Riley, and an Irish Catholic mother, how could I not be? There's no money in it – not much worth mentioning, anyway. I wouldn't exactly call it stealing; they are donation boxes, after all. More like my cut for the show we put on every week. Besides, I don't drink wine. Can't stand the smell or taste of it. The wine is all Harry's. I wish Father Dennis soaked the body of Christ in beer instead. I'm developing a taste for the amber fluid.

Dad's not too keen on Father Dennis. He refers to him as 'that Mick priest' and makes a point of getting his name wrong. He calls him David, Daniel, Peter, Luke, John – anything but Dennis. Dad says he's working his way through the Bible. It drives Mum mad.

I think Mum's keen on Father Dennis – she always looks forward to his visits every Tuesday for afternoon tea. He's not too old (doesn't use a walking stick) and is good looking (has all his teeth) in a priestly kind of way. Mum makes lamingtons every Tuesday. It's his favourite and mine too. Dad prefers to go to the pub on Tuesday afternoons. He doesn't like lamingtons.

That morning, I not only had to watch Kit do *my* altar duty, I also had to sit down the front of the church with Mum and Noni. It didn't take long until I dozed off. Latin does that to me.

'There are twenty-three brothels in Glebe and most of them in houses rented from the Church of England,' Father Dennis bellowed during his sermon. Everyone in the church sat bolt upright including me. When I told Dad about it afterwards, he reckoned it was because everyone was waiting for the addresses of the twenty-three brothels. He loves having a go at Catholics – it's his favourite pastime after gambling. Dad and Father Dennis are alike in one way: they both use any opportunity to have a go at the opposition. Problem is – they *are* the opposition. Dad says that having a go at the Church of England is Father Dennis's favourite pastime after bingo. Peas in a pod.

I spent a lazy Sunday afternoon learning how to throw darts with my left hand. The mouth-watering smell of Sunday roast sizzling away in the oven was making me hungry. I could have eaten a horse and chased the jockey, but it was only five o'clock. By the time dinner was ready, I was hitting bullseyes.

Our bread and dripping days are over now that Mum and Dad are making more money from their dressmaking and bookmaking businesses. With a belly full of food, I almost forgot about my broken arm. I didn't even feel like arguing with Noni, even though she can be a real pain in the neck. With the dishes done, Kit and I set up a game of Poker on the lounge-room floor – for matchsticks not money. We're in training for the big league – Dad's Friday card nights with his mates, where fortunes can be made and lost.

It was getting late, so we counted our matchsticks – thirty-seven to fifty-four – I won again. Just as I'd finished cheering, there was a loud banging on the door. *Who knocks on your front door at nine o'clock on a Sunday night?* I wondered. Kit and I looked at each other but didn't bother getting up. Mum and Dad were upstairs finishing off the books and tallying up their winnings from the Anniversary Day races. Finally Noni got up and threw her sewing on the lounge.

'You boys just lie there and play with matchsticks, why don't you? I've got to have this wedding dress finished by the end of the week. So I'll just stop sewing and answer the front door, shall I?' She stormed off up the hall.

'What's the matter with her?' Kit asked.

'Buggered if I know!' We quietly packed up the cards and matchsticks, and listened.

'Sorry to bother you, young lady. I'm Sergeant Bailey from Glebe Police Station. Are your parents home? I'd like a word with them.' I wasn't too alarmed. I had nothing to worry about – I had an alibi.

'Mum, Dad! The police want to talk to you,' Noni shouted up the stairs. I tried to stay cool, calm and collected. I moved along the carpet to hide my plaster cast behind the lounge. A precautionary move.

'What can we do for you?' Mum asked, breathlessly. 'Please come and sit down.' She led the way into the lounge room.

'This won't take long. I'll stand, if you don't mind.'

Dad entered, nodded at the sergeant, and then stood in front of the fireplace with his arm resting casually on the mantelpiece.

'There were some illegal goings-on in the neighbourhood yesterday. Anyone like to comment?' Sergeant Bailey looked around at us, one by one.

'I was taking care of the wife. She was laid up in bed all day with the flu. Had a few friends and family pop in to check on things. Nothing serious.'

Mum pulled out a hanky and blew her nose.

'Where were you boys?' Sergeant Bailey looked at me then at Kit, and then back to me. I knew better than to answer him.

'Joe was doing chores all day.' Dad was very convincing. He thought he was telling the truth.

'What about you, young man?'

Kit went bright red and started picking his nose. 'I went to the park ...'

'Were you at the billycart race?'

Kit looked to me for help but I was too busy building a tower out of the cards.

'I … um, I was there for a little while. I couldn't see anything, so I left.' Kit actually told a lie. I couldn't believe it!

Sergeant Bailey looked serious, like he was thinking hard about something. 'What did you do to your arm?'

I acted surprised at seeing my right arm in plaster. 'Oh, that. I fell off the sink. I was helping my sister put up some new curtains in the kitchen.' I felt positively angelic.

Sergeant Bailey looked at Noni to confirm my alibi. She nodded but didn't say anything. He scribbled something in his notebook and flicked back a couple of pages. I shot a quick glance at Dad. He was stony-faced, not giving anything away.

'Either of you boys know Harry Carter?'

Dad hit me across the ear. 'Answer the sergeant.'

'He's my best mate.'

'It appears Harry was at the billycart race.' Sergeant Bailey flipped over another page in his notebook. 'Two other witnesses reported some illegal gambling taking place. They say they placed bets on the race with a couple of young bookmakers. They're also claiming the race was rigged.' He flicked his notebook closed. 'You can have your billycart races, but no gambling and no taking bets. It's illegal. Do you understand?'

Kit and I nodded. We understood perfectly well that running books and taking bets is illegal – our father did it for a living. You could've heard a pin drop. We knew that we had a better chance of not getting caught if we kept our mouths shut.

'I'm going to let you boys off with a caution this time. If there's a next time, you won't be so lucky. Understood?'

'Leave it to me, Sergeant. There'll be no more shenanigans.' Dad glared at me like an eagle ready to swoop on its prey.

'I'll find my own way out. Good night and thank you for your time. Hope you're feeling better soon, Mrs Riley.' He nodded to Mum, turned to leave, and then stopped. 'If you hear anything about an illegal bookmaking business operating out of a house in the area, let me know. We've had an anonymous tip-off at the police station.'

'Will do,' replied Dad, putting both hands in his pockets. The sound of the front door shutting echoed through the house. Dad ripped off his belt. 'Get out the back, now! That was way too close for comfort.'

IT JUST ISN'T CRICKET

CHAPTER 6

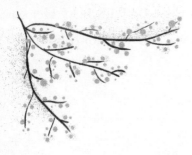

I'd had enough of Dad's beltings, and not just because of the welts on my backside and legs; it was the humiliation. I could stop him hitting Mum easy enough, but when he'd give me a belting, I'd just stand there like a stunned mullet, copping it.

I'm not putting up with it anymore, I decided. *I'm too old for this – I'm starting high school next week.*

The day after Sergeant Bailey's visit and my latest

belting, it was like nothing had happened: no threats, no belting, nothing. At supper, Dad looked almost happy.

'Your mother and I have been saving some of our hard-earned money and putting it into an education fund for you boys. Joe, you're the eldest, so you get first bite of the cherry. You're going to St Bartholomew's – to boarding school – congratulations, son!'

Dad shook my hand and then Mum hugged me. I didn't know what to say, I couldn't talk. I felt like the ground was cracking and I was falling into a deep crevice. I grabbed onto the table to steady myself and in a desperate attempt to avoid screaming, I shoved a whole piece of toast in my mouth.

Then, *wham!* Dad hit me across the head. 'Spit it out!' he shouted. I spat it right in his face. He grabbed me by the hair and pulled me to my feet.

'Stop it!' shouted Mum. This was my moment. The time had come. I lifted my right knee up, ramming it into his groin. He fell to his knees and rolled onto the floor, holding himself with both hands. I felt like kicking him again, but it just isn't cricket to kick someone when they're down, particularly your own father.

'Un … ungrate … ungrateful … little … bastard!'

'Apologise to your father.'

'Why should I? He almost pulled my hair out. I'm sick of him and I'm sick of his beltings.'

'He's your father!'

'You always stick up for him. Why do you do that? He hits you too.'

'We're wasting our money on that little bastard. He can go to the public school for all I care.'

'Fine with me,' I said.

'St Bart's will straighten him out, keep him out of trouble. He'll meet a better class of friend,' Mum said, adding insult to injury.

'I'm not going, and I don't need any other friends.'

'You'll do as your mother says. You'll go, alright!' It sounded more like a threat than an educational opportunity.

'I hate you, I hate both of you!' I ran upstairs to the bedroom that I shared with Kit, and locked the door. Throwing myself on the bed, I started punching my pillow and kept punching it until the feathers leaked out. I felt betrayed. I expected it from that bastard, but not from Mum. I kept asking myself: *Why does she want me to go? Who's going to break up their arguments when I'm not around?* Billy's getting too old; Kit's too young, too much of a wimp like I used to be.

'Joe, let me in!' It was Kit knocking on the door. My mind was racing – some kind of desperate madness was overtaking me: *I can run away to Uncle George's farm, live in one of his sheds, look after the chooks. No-one would ever find me there.*

'Mum wants to talk to you,' Kit called out. I couldn't hold back the tears any longer – I cried into my pillow so no-one could hear me.

'Joe?' It was Mum. 'Your father and I only want what's best for you. We've worked hard so that you boys can have a better start in life than we did. Please give it a go. Will you do that for me?'

My response was short, sharp and wounded: 'No!'

I got up from my bed and banged on the door. 'Go away!' I shouted. I needed time alone. My mind was still racing: *Why should I go away to boarding school when there's a perfectly good high school a few blocks away?* This was my home, I was born here, and so were Noni and Kit. So was Matilda, but she died nearly three years ago.

It makes me sad every time I think of her. She was only two weeks old, and never made it home from hospital. She had Kit's blue eyes, my ears and Noni's long fingers and toes. I'll never forget the funeral and the little white coffin in the horse-drawn carriage. It was covered with pink and white flowers. Everyone we knew was there. They formed a guard of honour from the park on the corner all the way to the church. We cried for days until Dad told us to shut up and get on with it – whatever that means. I've never seen Dad cry. Whenever anyone asks me how many brothers and sisters I have, I always say 'two sisters and one brother', because that's the truth.

'Joe, open the door – it's late – I've got to go to bed,' Kit said, banging on the door. There was no point delaying the inevitable, so I got up and unlocked the door then went back to bed. 'I don't want you to go away,' he said.

I was still too angry and upset to speak. 'Goodnight, Joe.'

I pretended to be asleep. I knew that it wasn't Kit's fault, but he wasn't the one being sent away to boarding school – I was.

THE OLD OAK TREE

TREE

CHAPTER 7

'You don't get it, do you, Joe? You're the lucky one. I wish I was going away to boarding school instead of having to stay home, making dresses and curtains, darning holes in smelly old socks, and sewing on buttons, hundreds of damn buttons. Mum and Dad have worked really hard to save money to send you to a good school and this is the thanks they get!' Noni was looking up into the tree, squinting, trying to find me and avoid the blinding rays of the late afternoon sun.

'They can keep their bloody money, I'm not going!' I said, looking down through the branches of the tree at the bottom half of Noni's pink and blue dress and her skinny white legs. 'He hates me! He wants to get rid of me!' I shouted.

'What do you expect after all the trouble you've caused? Dad could go to gaol if the police find out about his bookmaking business.'

'Who's going to protect Mum when I'm miles away at boarding school?'

'That's a bit rich! Most of the fights have been about you lately.'

'Piss off!'

'I'm telling Dad.'

'Yeah? And I'll tell Dad about your secret kissing and cuddling sessions in the backyard with what's-his-name every Saturday night.'

'You wouldn't dare!'

Kit climbed up the tree onto the branch below me. 'I don't want you to go,' he said. 'We won't win the cricket shield without you.' I can always rely on Kit to lift me up when I'm feeling down. 'Who's gonna keep

Chicka Barnes away from me? He wants to chop me up into little pieces and use me for bait!'

'He's just trying to scare you.'

'Have you seen the size of the fish he catches?'

Kit has a lot of growing up to do. *Maybe he'll grow up faster if I'm not here to look after him all the time*, I thought.

'I'll pick you up from school,' Noni called out. 'Chicka Barnes doesn't scare me. It'll give me a break from sewing.'

'But you're a girl! He'll pick on me even more if he sees me walking home with you. Nobody ever picks on me when Joe's around.'

'Please yourself, I've got work to do. Mrs Hargraves is collecting all of the dresses in the morning. The wedding's on Saturday. I hope it doesn't rain or the silk will be ruined.'

'I hope it pours and all the classrooms at St Bart's are flooded and the school is closed for good!' As soon as I started throwing acorns at Noni, Kit joined in.

'Ow! You little bastards!' She yelled, running towards the back door. 'I'm telling Dad. You'll get a belting for this!'

'Hey Joe, you'll miss out on Dad's beltings while you're away,' said Kit. 'Maybe boarding school won't be so bad after all.'

Always the optimist – he drives me mad sometimes.

'You think so? Harry says they use a bull whip on the boys at St Bart's.' Kit looked alarmed. 'They'll have to catch me first!' I said, as I swung down onto the branch next to him. We sat and watched the sun set then waited for the full moon to appear above the rooftops.

It's the same tree I've been climbing and the same moon I've been watching for as long as I can remember. It's where I'd come to hide from Dad and to dream of other places I might go, things I might do, people I might meet. I could've stayed up there in that old oak tree all night, staring at the moon all night. You can't do that with the sun, you'd go blind.

'Hello moon,' I said to myself. That was how I'd greeted it ever since I was a little boy. I didn't feel much like that boy anymore.

LEAVING

I couldn't get to sleep – my mind was racing and my head was spinning. My business empire was being destroyed and I couldn't do anything about it.

Joe and Harry's Extra Large Farm Fresh Eggs – twenty shillings a week. Harry said: 'No problem, easy enough to get rid o' "Joe" from the business name – a slap o' paint should do the trick. I'll just hafta catch the train out to Rooty Hill by meself to pick up the eggs.' *He's big enough and ugly enough to do that*, I thought.

'A piece o' cake!' he said. 'And I get to keep all the profit.' *Good ol' best friend, Harry.*

My paper run – three shillings a week. Kit wants to take it over but he's only ten years old. Harry's too busy with the egg business and helping his dad with odd jobs. *Not that bloody new kid from Cowra! Over my dead body!*

Altar duty – two shillings a week. Not technically a business but it keeps me in cigarettes. Father Dennis said I'll be a hard act to follow. *That was the best he could come up with after three years of dedicated service?*

I hadn't even left and I was already the spare leg, the old billycart, the has-been. All that work down the drain.

That night I dreamt about a tall man in a black hooded robe and shiny black shoes who was chasing me between rows of desks and then down a long, white, deserted corridor into a classroom that only had one door, no windows, no way out. I was trapped. He got closer and closer until he was towering over me. As he raised his arm, light reflected off the long metal object he was holding. His hood fell back – he had no face! I screamed and woke myself up.

I looked across at Kit's bed, but Kit wasn't there. I sat up in bed in front of the open window. The leaves on the old oak tree were rustling in the cool breeze, but I was sweating. The sun was rising and burning off each cloud, one by one. It was going to be another scorcher.

I took off my pyjamas and threw them into the open suitcase on the floor. It was really happening – I was leaving home, leaving everything I'd loved and worked for. I was going away to St Bart's – St Bartholomew's College for Boys. My prized possessions were in that case: a cricket ball (courtesy of Don Bradman's bat at the Sydney Cricket Ground), rosary beads (a present from Mum for my Holy Communion), three blue ribbons for athletics (first over fifty yards, three years in a row), a family photograph (I cut Dad out; he wasn't smiling anyway) and five pounds, ten shillings and sixpence.

There was a pile of things on the end of my bed still to pack: spare shirt and socks, sandshoes, satchel, underwear, new comb and toothbrush. I threw them into the case, closed the lid and did up the metal clips. I looked at the school uniform hanging on the wardrobe door and snarled: a woollen blazer with a stupid school crest on the pocket, a blue shirt, and a red, blue and gold striped tie with another stupid crest. Laid out on the chair were grey woollen shorts and socks with more stupid red, blue and gold stripes. Polished black school shoes were under the chair, while a hat (with stupid red, blue and gold striped ribbon) was hanging on the back.

'I can't do this!' I said, looking at myself in the mirror. I'd become a spectator in my own life. I was shivering. I couldn't stand there naked all morning, someone might see me. After kicking my case around the room, I got dressed into my uniform, except for the stupid blazer and tie.

'Breakfast is ready!' called Mum.

Suddenly Kit ran in, spear-tackling me. 'Rumble time!' he shouted.

I fell, broken-arm-first onto the floor. 'Idiot!'

'Come on, one more wrestle before you go!'

Grabbing onto each other, we rolled from side to side on the floor, both trying to get the upper hand. The little monkey was getting stronger. Finally, he forced his way on top of me, almost in control, when I took a deep breath and, with every ounce of strength I had, pushed him off, pinning him down. I wasn't about to lose a wrestle with my little brother.

Looking him in the eyes, I thought: *God, I'm going to miss you!* I let him go and called it a tie then ran downstairs with Kit right on my tail.

Mum was in a flap. She wasn't making much sense. 'How will they know you like your bacon soft or your sausages crisp or your eggs well done? Maybe there are no eggs? It's the Depression, after all …' Mum rambled on and on, and at the same time managed to pack a string bag with enough biscuits, cakes and fruit to feed the whole family for a week. Food was the least of my worries but I knew I'd never win that argument.

Dad shook hands with me at the front door. 'Goodbye son. Do us proud.' That was it from Dad. Kit and I had a secret handshake that ended with a big bear hug and growl. Noni kissed me on the cheek and messed up my hair. I was going to miss them all, maybe even Dad eventually.

GETTING THERE

Mum talked all the way to the tram stop but when we finally got on the tram she went quiet. I looked out the window as we rattled along Glebe Point Road past the post office, Donato's fish shop, the general store, Uncle Les and Aunt Lil's greengrocers, Mr Thompson's paper shop and four pubs, stopping every couple of blocks to drop off and pick up passengers. We turned left onto Parramatta Road where the abbey used to be before it was moved stone by stone to Bridge

Road a few years ago. The tram picked up speed as it headed downhill onto Broadway, stopping at Grace Bros and then Railway Square, where a lot of people were queued outside one of the buildings.

'They're all out of work,' said Mum, 'waiting to collect their susso – you know, relief money and food, just like we had to for a little while. Remember when I picked up those vouchers from the booths at Circular Quay and then walked all the way down here? Nearly two miles – makes no sense. You can't afford tram fares when you're on susso. Most of those poor sods would've had to walk from home in the first place.'

It felt strange sitting on a tram in my private school uniform watching poor, unemployed people queuing to pick up food and money to stay alive.

The tram took off again down George Street, past more shops (some of them boarded up), a theatre, pubs on nearly every corner, Anthony Hordern's department store, up to Woolworths, the Town Hall, the Queen Victoria Building and more boarded-up buildings and closed banks, and then past the GPO and Martin Place until we arrived at the Circular Quay ferry terminal.

We caught a ferry that went under the Harbour Bridge. They started building the bridge when I was eight years old. It still wasn't finished, just the big arch. There's going to be a roadway, railway tracks and footpaths all hanging from the arch. It'll be one of the wonders of the world.

The ferry chugged past a long row of wharves and ships being loaded and unloaded. Mum pulled a booklet out of her bag and started reading it. I looked over her shoulder – 'Prospectus' – whatever that means. It was all about St Bart's: 'Catholic boys only will be accepted. Preference will be given to boys with academic and/or athletic ability. Donations gratefully accepted.' There's no way that Mum and Dad would've made a donation to the school. That left two out of four. *St Bart's must be desperate*, I thought.

When we arrived, I felt like I was walking the plank off the ferry, about to jump into deep water and left to drown. There was no-one waiting to get on, and Mum and I were the only ones to get off. Water splashed up through the holes in the rotting timber wharf as the ferry took off again. We followed a stone wall all the way up a steep hill. The sun was getting higher and hotter. 'I've got blisters, I hate these shoes!' I said, kicking the stone wall.

'Stop that! Look what you've done to your new shoes,' Mum whispered, looking embarrassed. I'd scuffed the leather on the toes and my blisters were hurting even more. She looked really hot and bothered but kept walking. The stone wall seemed to be going on forever until I saw two enormous sandstone pillars at the front gates. As I stopped to read the sign, Mum grabbed my arm and pulled me inside. We were late.

We joined a crowd of people waiting on a large circle of lawn. I suddenly felt like a small fish in a big pond. The loud hum of voices went quiet as soon as a tall man wearing a long black robe and a ridiculous hat tapped on a microphone, making it screech. *That's him – that's the man from my dream!* I said to myself. He stood proudly behind a lectern that was set up on the verandah between sandstone columns.

'Good morning parents, teachers and students. Welcome to St Bartholomew's College. I am Monsignor Reynolds, the head of this esteemed college for Catholic boys. We are embarking on a journey together in which we will instil strong Catholic beliefs and principles by which all men can live, whatever their chosen path in life. This morning's proceedings will commence with Mass in the school chapel followed by morning tea on the lawn around our magnificent rose garden. All boys are expected to help in serving tea to their parents and other special guests. At twelve o'clock, students will bid their farewells then assemble outside the Great Hall. Brother Felix will now lead us to Mass.'

We all squeezed inside a chapel about half the size of St James's at Glebe. I watched with a critical eye as four senior boys assisted on the altar. They were not as good as I'd expected: a little stiff and a bit too solemn. Amateurs. Boring! I looked around the chapel – no donation boxes that I could see.

After I helped serve morning tea in the rose garden, it was time for Mum and the other parents to leave. 'Goodbye, Joe. I'll miss you,' she said, her lip trembling.

'I'll miss you too.'

'Before you know it, you'll be back home for the

holidays,' she said, sniffing and wiping away the tears rolling down her cheeks with the hanky she'd been clutching. 'Do you have your rosary beads?'

'They're right here,' I said, putting my hand over my heart and blazer pocket. Then I gave Mum a big hug, but forgot about my broken arm. I almost knocked her over with my plaster cast. My eyes started to water and my throat felt dry.

'That sun is really bright,' I said, rubbing my eyes. Mum smiled at my pathetic excuse and squeezed my hand. I tried hard to be strong. My tears were trapped inside for a more private time.

ORIENTATION

I sleep in a dorm – that's boarding school talk for dormitory – with nineteen other boys. It's like a hospital but without the doctors and nurses. I have a single bed, two drawers and a coat hanger. The blankets look like they were left over from the Great War but my bedspread looks new. There's a bathroom at one end of the dorm with concrete walls and floor, which I'm told, makes it easy to hose down. The communal shower has no taps, five shower heads and cold water only. *There was no mention of that in the Prospectus.* I can't complain as that's pretty much the situation at home where we have to boil the kettle every time we want hot water. Showers are in one-minute shifts with two bars of soap between five boys.

Brother Sebastian watches us from a dry distance, controlling the tap, barking orders and giving helpful advice like: 'Under the shower – don't be shy – don't waste water – it's only cold if you think it's cold – ten seconds to go.'

At my first shower, I tried thinking hot but the water stayed cold. *I hate to think what it's going to be like here in winter. With any luck, I'll be home by then,* I thought, shivering under the cold water.

Every morning to wake us up, Brother Sebastian walks through the junior dorms ringing a loud bell and turning on the lights. The keen ones jump out of bed and are kneeling down and praying by the time he gets back.

'Out of bed the rest of you! Get cracking!'

When he calls out the morning drill, it's a race against time: pray, make bed, go to the dunny, get dressed, polish shoes, pack satchel, run to Mass, eat breakfast (a large bowl of cold, lumpy porridge), clear tables, wash or wipe up (see kitchen roster), assemble in the Great Hall, go to class.

Orientation on the first two days was hard work, but nothing compared to my initiation. While two senior prefects held me upside down over a dunny, another prefect with a bad breath problem yelled in my ear: 'What are the three Rs?' When I didn't answer, Bad Breath yelled at me again.

I knew it was a trick question but I had to say something. 'Reading, Riting—' But before I could say 'Rithmetic, one of them pulled the chain and the water from the cistern flushed all around my head. I tried to scream, but swallowed water instead. I was thrashing about and kept hitting my head on the porcelain.

When the water cleared, I coughed and spluttered to the sound of: 'Rowing, Rugby, Running!' The problem was, I couldn't make out exactly what they were saying until after the third flush. I can vouch for the fact that being held upside down does nothing to help your brain work any faster. I took Brother

Sebastian's advice and tried to imagine that the water was warm. That didn't work either. When I finally managed to say, 'Rowing, Rugby, Running,' my torturers cheered, helping me to my feet. I was officially a St Bart's boy.

The prefects do a lot more than initiations. They run rackets – they're standover men who expect and take bribes. Cash, cigarettes and food are all legal tender if you want to avoid detention or six cuts of the cane for dirty shoes, crooked ties, hair parted on the wrong side, hair not parted, hat worn at the wrong angle and the list goes on. Thank God for the cakes Mum sends me in a food parcel every week because my hard-earned money would've been fast disappearing.

The night after my initiation, I dreamt that I was trapped underwater in a deep, dark well. I could see the wall of the well but couldn't touch it. I kicked hard, trying to swim to the surface, but it was too far. I couldn't reach it. I was drowning – it was terrifying. I screamed, waking up Brother Sebastian and the other boys in my dormitory, earning myself a Saturday detention.

AMDG
CHAPTER 11

The only seat left in English was in the front row. I'd never sat up the front before and I wasn't keen to start. As soon as I sat down, I came face to face with Brother Thomas, who's about the same height as Noni. His name was written in large, perfectly formed letters on the blackboard, and there was an amazing coloured chalk drawing of Jesus in the top left-hand corner of the board, just below the letters AMDG.

'In the name of the Father, Son and Holy Ghost, let

us pray.' Brother Thomas said, bowing his head, and I did the same. Two minutes seemed like two hours. 'In the name of the Father, Son and Holy Ghost, Amen.'

'Amen,' we all mumbled.

'Open your exercise books and write AMDG on the top line.' Brother Thomas walked around, checking that everyone had written it properly. 'Does anybody know what AMDG stands for?' Not a hand went up, but there were a few grins and knowing looks. 'It's not "Auntie Mary's Dead Goat", if that's what some of you are thinking.' There was lots of snickering. Brother Thomas grabbed his cane and whacked it on my desk. 'Stop that!' he yelled, glaring at me and the other culprits. I felt a bit of his spit land on my right cheek. As he pointed his cane and hit each of the four letters on the blackboard, he said: '*Ad maiorem Dei gloriam*. You should all know what this means.'

It's supposed to be an English class, I thought. I don't know why, but I put up my hand.

'Yes, Master Riley,' he said, smiling encouragement.

I wondered how he knew my name – I'd only been at the school two days. 'It's Latin, sir.'

'Good observation. Do you know what the English translation is?'

'Something to do with God, sir?' It was a gift.

'It means "For the greater glory of God", which, as all of you should know, is our school motto. You must write AMDG at the top of every page in your exercise books to remind you that your schoolwork is dedicated to the glory of God.'

When I wrote AMDG on the top line of the next page, I had to say 'Auntie Mary's Dead Goat' to myself so that I got the letters in the right order.

'You'll all need your dictionaries for the next task. I want you to look up your full name – your Christian name and your surname – in your dictionary. When you've found both names, close your dictionary and sit up straight with your arms folded.' Brother Thomas sat down at his desk, opened up a book called *Great Expectations* and started reading it.

I opened my dictionary and looked in the Js for Joe. It wasn't there. I looked down the page for 'Joseph' – not there either. Then I looked up 'Riley' and found 'rile'. *Is that close enough?* I thought. I put up my hand.

Two other boys had their hands up as well. Brother Thomas must've been up to a really exciting part in his book because he kept reading. I coughed to try and get his attention – it did the trick. He looked up and pointed to the boy with his hand up next to me.

'Your name?'

'Maurice MacDonald, sir, but everyone calls me Mac.'

'We don't use nicknames at St Bartholomew's. Yes, Master MacDonald?'

'There are no names or proper nouns in an English dictionary, sir.'

'Well done!'

'I've checked twice but I can't find "superantidisestablishmentarianism". It's the longest word in the world. We need bigger dictionaries, sir.'

'Did I ask you to look up the longest word in the world?' Brother Thomas grabbed Mac's copy of the *Concise Oxford Dictionary* and hit him on the back of the head with it.

Doesn't pay to be too smart at St Bart's.

'No, sir.'

'That, Master MacDonald, was a rhetorical question. Do you know what a rhetorical question is?'

'No, sir.'

'Then you're not as smart as you think you are.' Brother Thomas wrote 'rhetorical' on the blackboard. 'Everyone, look up "rhetorical" in your dictionaries. Raise your hand as soon as you've found it.' Brother Thomas sat back down and kept reading his book. I was still going through the Rs when the bell sounded for the end of the first period.

At this rate, my vocabulary is going to improve rapidly, I thought.

RULES

CHAPTER 12

There are so many rules to learn at St Bart's: dorm rules, chapel rules, assembly rules, dining hall rules, uniform rules, classroom rules, house rules, library rules. On day three, I made it through most of the morning drill, but 'most' isn't good enough. I got the cane for not folding my pyjamas and not making my bed to dorm standard, and then scored extra kitchen duty for being late to rostered wiping up.

Jumping on beds is forbidden (dorm rule 23), but great fun. At the end of the first week, I could run across the twenty beds in my dorm in under ten seconds, a new dorm record.

I'm not used to wearing a school uniform every day. At Glebe Public, no-one got the cane or detention for wearing the wrong colour shirt, shorts or socks. Ties were optional and blazers were unheard of. At St Bart's, I even get the cane when my socks aren't pulled up and folded over so their red, blue and gold stripes can be seen. There are also exceptions to some of the rules. Blazers must be worn at all times but taken off in class. We must take our hats off before entering the chapel, library, classrooms and dining hall, but keep them on in Assembly, except when saying prayers and singing hymns. And I keep forgetting to doff my hat when walking past prefects, teachers and anyone else worthy of a doff. It gets me an afternoon detention every time. At this rate, I'll be spending more time in detention than in class.

Mealtimes aren't much fun either. It's not just the lousy food, but the strict rules on how to eat it. If I even think about using my fingers, the cane comes crashing down on them out of nowhere. We're supposed to cut everything up into small pieces and chew each bit at least six times before swallowing, even mashed potato. I defy anyone to eat peas by pushing them on the back of their fork, like we've been told to do. Some of the meals are really bad, but the worst is boiled tripe in a yellow glue-like sauce with cabbage that's boiled to within an inch of its life, boiled turnips or chokos (it's impossible to tell which), and the compulsory runny mashed potato that's slopped on the plate. I'd never appreciated the art of food presentation until I came to St Bart's.

I stopped getting any sympathy for my broken arm after the first week, except from Brother Felix, my Arithmetic teacher. He was on my case from day one. 'I can't read your numbers. Is that a three or a five? Can't you write properly? That's wrong – that's wrong – that's wrong! Can't you add up? Stop smudging ink everywhere! Your work is a disgrace!'

I tried telling him that I'm right-handed (and my right forearm is obviously broken) but he wouldn't listen. When I tried writing with my left hand, it just wouldn't work. It was hard writing with my right hand because the plaster is so heavy and kept getting in the way. I could've been plastered from head to toe and it wouldn't have made a scrap of difference to Brother Felix. There are no excuses for any work that is less than perfect. Every Arithmetic lesson, that mongrel gives me a sixer. Like everyone else, I get to choose my preferred method of punishment: the cane or the leather strap that's clipped to the rosary beads around his waist. I always pick the cane – no-one's going to belt me with a leather strap ever again. If they even try, they're going to get the same treatment I gave Dad.

The last time I got the cane from Brother Felix, I held out my left hand ready for it.

'Bend over!' he shouted. I bent over a bit but not far enough. He pushed my head lower, giving me a sixer on the backside. I wondered if he had second thoughts about using the cane on my hands because of my broken arm. He's the only teacher who ever orders us to bend over to get the cane. He gets this weird look on his face, like he's angry and enjoying it at the same time. A real sicko if you ask me. I'm not sure how much longer I can put up with being caned on the backside by a grown man, Brother or no Brother.

BLOOD BROTHERS

I can count the friends I've made on two fingers. The rest may as well be from another planet. The Martians, I call them – they talk with plums in their mouths, walk with brooms up their bums, and look down on boys like me from the wrong side of town. They don't need to work hard to get ahead – they've got their inheritances to fall back on.

Just because someone's got more money and lives in a big house that's not rented from the Church of England, doesn't mean they're a better person, even if they are what Mum calls a 'better class of friend'. I don't get this whole 'class' thing. There are poor people and rich people, and a whole lot in between trying either to get rich or to just put food on the table and make ends meet.

Mac is one of my new mates. His family lives in a mansion on Sydney Harbour with a housekeeper, gardener, swimming pool and a car. Mac never brags about being rich; he seems more embarrassed about it. He's not like the Martians at all.

Teddy Foster is my other new mate. He's really different to anyone else I've ever met. He comes from a cattle station in Queensland and isn't used to going to school, wearing shoes, or sitting still on a chair for very long, unless of course he's eating. Teddy loves food. He even eats my leftover tripe and then looks around for more. He'd much rather be sitting in a saddle and rounding up cattle than sitting behind a school desk all day.

Teddy, Mac and I sleep three in a row in the dorm – just like the Three Bears. That's what the Martians call us because we always stick together. Teddy's the tallest and Mac's the shortest, so I'm in the middle. We walk together, talk together, eat together, pray together, study together and play sport together. We were on the same cricket team until Brother Thomas, who's also the cricket coach, split us up for talking too much. I couldn't bat or bowl properly with my arm in plaster but I could catch a ball, no problem, with my left hand.

One afternoon behind the sport shed, Mac, Teddy and I pricked our fingers and exchanged blood – we were officially blood brothers. I'd do anything for Mac and Teddy, and they'd do anything for me.

There's a common study area at the end of our dorm where we have desks and are supervised by Brother Sebastian every afternoon and evening, before and after dinner. Mac's a whiz at Arithmetic, Spelling and Latin, and is only very good at every other subject. He always finishes his homework while I'm still stuck on the first page of sums. But since we've become blood brothers, Mac's been 'helping' me with my

Arithmetic. When he finishes his work, we check to see that Brother Sebastian isn't looking then swap our exercise books. Mac can write numbers just like me, and just like Teddy as well. We've worked out some hand signals to use in class, like deaf people do. It's too risky to try and swap exercise books in Arithmetic because Brother Felix would be onto us straight away – he has eyes in the back of his head.

Mum and Dad are going to be very impressed with my Arithmetic marks if we can manage to keep this up. I'd get Mac to do some of my other homework as well if I could. The trouble is – his handwriting is worse than mine.

ANGELS

I'd been an altar boy back home at Glebe for nearly three years, but not as long as Mac. Teddy never had the chance, living in the outback. It's two hundred miles to the nearest church and even then it's Presbyterian.

Mac and I were excited about being chosen to be altar boys at St Bart's until we found out that Brother Felix takes altar practice. On our first afternoon, the chapel was stinking hot with the sun beating down on us through the west-facing windows. I could feel sweat spreading out from my armpits and running down my back. Brother Felix locked the chapel doors to keep the heat out, but it wasn't working.

'Follow me to the vestry. You can get changed into your robes straight away,' he said, marching past the altar like a general leading his troops. The vestry is a cool but badly lit room with a wardrobe, chest of drawers, an armchair and a full-length mirror. We stood on the rug in the middle of the room, waiting for further orders, while Brother Felix picked out robes and surplices from the wardrobe. 'Blazers, shirts, shorts off, and then put these on,' he said, giving each of us a black robe and a white surplice to go over the top.

I looked at Mac and the other two boys, Mick and Frank. Like them, I couldn't wait to get my hot school clothes off, but I'd always worn more than underwear under my robe. We shrugged at each other then started getting undressed. I was having trouble pulling my blazer sleeve over the cast, so Brother Felix helped me. Then he undid my tie and started undoing the buttons on my shirt.

'Chin up, boy!' He said, standing very close to me. Too close. I was starting to feel uncomfortable. When he undid the zipper on my shorts, I jumped back in fright. 'Stand still, I'm only trying to help!' This was the same Brother Felix who showed no mercy in Arithmetic, all of a sudden wanting to help me get undressed. He looked at me in a weird way as his hand brushed against the front of my underpants. It was no accident. Out of the corner of my eye, I saw Frank almost fall over trying to get his shorts off before Brother Felix moved onto his zipper.

Altar practice went well after that and Brother Felix even congratulated me on my technique. Maybe I'd imagined that light touch. Then again, there was that look in his eyes.

'Of course it was an accident!' Mac said afterwards. 'Why would he want to touch you there, of all places? Doctors might do that sort of thing but not Priests or Brothers.' Mac made a lot of sense. I put it to the back of my mind.

We stripped off again the following week. Sydney was having its worst heatwave in years. Brother Felix helped me undress but this time kept his distance. It was Mick who was singled out for special attention. After practice, Brother Felix asked him to stay back for another five minutes, just to go over a few moves. 'I'll see the rest of you next week.'

When we walked into the chapel the following week, Brother Felix was nowhere in sight. We found him sitting on the armchair in the vestry waiting for us. He'd given Mac and Frank the afternoon off, as he said that Mick and I needed more practice.

'Come here,' he said.

Mick and I moved closer to him.

'Kneel down.'

As we knelt in front of him, he placed a hand on each of our heads. I waited for him to bless us, but he didn't. When he took his hand off my head, I looked up and saw him put it under his robe. He looked like he was scratching himself. His other hand was on Mick's head.

Suddenly I felt sick in the stomach. I could feel my

lunchtime tripe rising up. It kept coming and I couldn't stop it. I threw up all over Brother Felix.

'You disgusting creature!' he yelled, pushing me away. I fell onto my broken arm but it didn't hurt anymore. Brother Felix was a real mess, and the smell was awful. The half-digested tripe was dripping down his black robe. I felt like running away but I threw up again instead.

'Get out of my sight!' he said between clenched teeth.

Mick helped me to my feet and as soon as we were outside the chapel, he patted me on the back. 'Perfect timing, old boy – couldn't have done it better myself!' Mick seems to take everything in his stride. His father is an admiral in the Navy. A chip off the old block.

I was sick as a dog. Mick almost had to carry me to the infirmary. Sister Monica, the school nurse, helped me onto the bed and took my shoes off. She propped up some pillows behind me and held a glass of cold water for me to sip. She felt my forehead, shook a thermometer and then put it in my mouth. I watched a fan spinning around on the ceiling and felt a bit better with the cool air blowing on my face.

'Can I get the plaster off soon, Sister? It's real itchy.'

Sister Monica pulled a card out of the box on her desk and checked it. It's ready to come off, alright.' I watched as she cut the plaster, lifting it off in one piece. I looked at my thin, pale arm. 'You'll be back on the cricket pitch in no time!' she said.

I must've fallen asleep because the next thing I knew the bell was ringing for dinner. *I could get used to this,* I thought.

'Are you awake?' It was Sister Monica. She felt my forehead. 'You're burning up. You'll have to stay here overnight.' She gave me some more medicine and a glass of water to wash it down.

My eyelids started to feel heavier and heavier. *I love Sister Monica,* I thought, *she's an angel sent from heaven.*

I dreamt that I was in Brother Felix's Arithmetic class. He was banging on my desk with his fist, carrying on about my mistakes and ink blots, when *blah!* I threw up all over him. Then I was in the chapel in the middle of altar practice. He pushed me to my knees, and when he put his hand on my head, I threw up all over his shiny black shoes.

I was sick for another two days.

BACK HOME

I wasn't feeling sick anymore – I was homesick. If it hadn't been for Mac, Teddy and Sister Monica, I don't know what I would've done. I started having nightmares, the same one every night. A man wearing a dark robe walks into Mum and Dad's bedroom, holding a knife. He leans over Mum, who is sleeping. He raises his arm, ready to stab her. I scream, a blood-curdling scream. Mac and Teddy wake me up, slapping me on the face to snap me out of it. It's terrifying – it seems so real. I've started worrying about Mum all the time.

There were two more weeks until Easter, but I didn't think I could last that long. *There must be something wrong with me*, I thought, *not to mention Brother Felix. There's something seriously wrong with him. I haven't done anything to be ashamed of, but I feel like I have. I don't know what to do!* Then it came to me in a flash: *I'll go home – just for the weekend – Mac and Teddy will cover for me. We're blood brothers after all.*

It was easy. On Friday afternoon after sport, I just walked out. I caught the ferry to Circular Quay and then the tram back to Glebe.

It was five o'clock, and I was pretty sure that Dad would still be at the pub. The front door was wide open. Mum was in the kitchen and nearly jumped out of her skin when she saw me.

'Surprise!' I said, giving her a big hug then lifting her up and swinging her around.

'What are you doing home?' she asked. I tried not to make eye contact. Mum is a walking, talking lie detector.

'This weekend is "home weekend" for all the new boys – all the new altar boys, like me!'

'You're an altar boy at St Bart's? Congratulations, Joe!' Mum kissed me hard on the cheek. My lie was working a treat. As she looked me up and down, my right eye started to quiver.

'You're so thin. Are you getting enough to eat? There's a meatloaf in the oven.' Mum was very excited to have me home.

'You wouldn't believe the muck they feed us – tripe at least twice a week, and more kidney, liver and brains than anything else. I give all that rubbish to Teddy to eat – he's one of my new mates. It's no wonder I've lost weight!'

'It's a disgrace! With the money we're paying, they should be feeding you lamb or steak.' Mum stood at the stove, stirring a pot. 'When do you have to be back at school?' she asked.

'Sunday night,' I replied, looking down at my shoes – they were still shiny from their morning polish. Then I set the table without being asked.

'Where's your bag?' she asked, with that look on her face. *The game's just about up,* I thought.

I heard the front door close, and then footsteps

in the hall. 'What are you doing home?' Noni asked, giving me a quick peck on the cheek, looking pleased to see me.

Kit was right behind her. We did our secret handshake, finishing with an extra loud growl. 'Mr Thompson let me take over your paper run. Doesn't seem to mind that I'm only ten – saves him money he says. Did you hear about the crook that's been bashing paperboys and stealing their money? If he comes near me, I'll knock him down, kick him in the nuts—'

'You'll do no such thing, Christopher Riley!'

Kit ignored Mum and kept going. 'I'll tie his hands behind his back, then push and shove him all the way to the police station. When he falls over, I'll lay my boot into him like this—'

'That's enough!' said Mum. She needn't have worried – Kit could only ever hurt someone in his dreams.

'Did you hear about what happened in Church?' Noni asked, with a twinkle in her eye.

'Why don't you mind your own business?' Kit snapped.

'If you don't tell him, I will.'

'Tell me what?' I asked.

Kit rolled his eyes and sighed. 'Father Dennis asked me to be an altar boy, a proper one like you. I was running late and in too much of a rush to notice that I'd put my robe on inside out. I followed Father Dennis up the altar steps and went one step too far. When he opened the little curtain to put the body of Christ inside, one of the other altar boys pulled the back of my robe and I nearly fell down the steps. People started laughing. Then I smelt the incense burning – it always makes me sneeze. I couldn't stop. After Mass, Father Dennis got really angry with me. I'm not an altar boy anymore.'

I put my arm around Kit. 'Being an altar boy isn't everything it's cracked up to be.'

'Dinner's ready!' Mum said, putting the plates on the table.

I heard a key trying to find the lock in the front door. The door flew open, banging against the wall.

'Well, look who's here!' Dad said, drunk as usual, but trying his best in front of Mum to look sober. Mum pushed past him with the plates. He lost his balance and fell against the table. 'Is it holidays already? Time flies when you're having fun.' Dad pulled out his chair, just managing to sit on it without falling off. 'Good to have you home, son.' He tucked into his dinner straight away.

'Joe, would you like to say grace?' Mum asked, ignoring Dad's bad manners.

'For the food we are about to eat, thank you, Lord. Amen.' I couldn't wait to tuck in myself. We ate quietly like we always do. Dad doesn't like talking at the dinner table – says it gives him indigestion.

As soon as Dad was finished, he pulled a newspaper out of his back pocket and studied the racing guide. Mum cleared the table and Noni started washing up. Kit and I were supposed to be wiping up, but we spent more time flicking each other with our wet tea towels. After dinner, we all sat around the kitchen table listening to the wireless. Everything was just how it should be. I went to bed happy for the first time in ages.

THE GAME'S UP

*W*ho knocks on your front door at six o'clock on a Saturday morning? Too early for Dad's punters, I thought. I stuck my head out the bedroom window but couldn't hear anything. Kit was lying across from me in his bed, sound asleep.

'Mum, Dad, there's a priest here to see you!' There was no mistaking Noni's voice – even the neighbours can hear her when she shouts up the stairs.

Please God, let it be Father Dennis at the front door,

I prayed. I'm all for praying – I need all the help I can get.

I saw Mum run past my bedroom door in her dressing gown. I followed her halfway down the stairs, stopping when I heard a familiar voice:

'Good morning, Mrs Riley. Sorry to bother you at this hour of the morning. Joseph went missing from St Bartholomew's late yesterday. I believe he may have come home.'

The game's up.

'What's going on?' Dad called out from the top of the stairs. I wanted to run, but couldn't decide which direction was best. With Dad behind me and the Monsignor blocking my way to the front door, running away wasn't an option. A voice inside me said: *Be a man – stand your ground and fight – no plaster cast to hold you back anymore.* But who was I kidding? I didn't stand a chance. I decided to hide in my bedroom until I could think things through. I turned around and ran upstairs as fast as I could.

'Where are you going?' Dad asked as I ran past him and into my bedroom, locking the door. I thought about jumping out the window but the twenty-foot drop onto the garden path wasn't a good idea. I'd get more than a broken arm for my trouble and I wasn't about to get any more plaster on my body if I could help it.

'What are you doing?' Kit asked sleepily, rubbing his eyes.

'I've got to go back to St Bart's.'

'That's not fair!' Kit cried out, pulling the covers up over his head.

I threw my school clothes onto the floor, kicking them around the room, planning my attack. 'Rumble time!' I shouted, jumping on Kit's bed and tickling him. When he tried to push me off, I grabbed onto him then we fell on the floor, wrestling and laughing. I soon got the upper hand, but when I looked in his eyes, I didn't feel like a winner. I got dressed slowly into my school uniform.

As soon as I walked into the lounge room, Dad slapped me across the face. 'You've put the Monsignor to a lot of trouble, and you've lied to us again. What have you got to say for yourself?'

The Monsignor stepped in between Dad and me.

'This is a school matter, Mr Riley, and I will deal with Joseph personally back at St Bartholomew's. Sorry to trouble you. We must get back in time for Mass.'

Mum was crying. 'Is anything the matter, Joe? Is there something you're not telling us?'

'He hasn't told the truth – that's what he hasn't told us!' Dad was so angry, he was shaking.

Maybe going back to St Bart's is the best option after all, I thought.

Monsignor Reynolds cleared his throat. 'Mrs Riley, trying to make excuses for Joseph's selfish actions will only prolong the problem. He needs discipline – the kind of discipline that we know best how to provide at St Bartholomew's.'

Dad was nodding but didn't look like he was agreeing with what the Monsignor was saying.

'What discipline? He must've just walked out the school gate! With the school fees I'm paying, I expect you to look after my son properly and not let him roam the streets of Sydney at all hours of the day and night. Anything could've happened to him.' Dad always likes to have the last word.

After we said our goodbyes, I followed the Monsignor into the front seat of his car, a 1928 Ford Model A Rumble Seat Roadster. It goes up to sixty-five miles an hour, twenty more than the Model T, and purrs like a kitten. We could've just as easily caught the tram and ferry like Mum and I did, but I was glad we didn't. It was magic sitting in the front seat, looking out the window and watching shops being opened, windows cleaned and footpaths hosed down, ready for the day's business. The trams were almost empty – the city was still coming to life. Ours was the only car going west across the Iron Cove Bridge. There was more action in the water, with ferries and fishing boats coming and going in all directions. I wound down the window for a better look. The smoky breeze filled my lungs as we sped up Victoria Road towards St Bart's. Monsignor Reynolds concentrated on driving and didn't speak to me the whole way there.

After all that talk about discipline, I got off lightly: six cuts of the cane on each hand, then off to confession to repent my sins. My penance – two lousy rosaries. Twenty Our Fathers and a hundred Hail

Marys later, I was a new man. Not bad for a night back home with the family and a ride in one of the best cars you can buy. Well worth the trouble, whichever way I looked at it.

NEWS
CHAPTER 17

I've been suspended from altar boy duty for four weeks – *not long enough, if you ask me.* I told Brother Felix that I didn't need any help getting undressed and if he touched me again, even accidentally, I'd tell Monsignor Reynolds everything. It kind of did the trick – Brother Felix suspended me for insolence – sounds like a disease.

I worked out that it was one week, four days, nine hours and thirty-seven minutes since I'd been for a ride in the 1928 Ford Model A Roadster dream machine.

Mum's cottage by the sea will have to wait until after I buy a car like that, I thought. *Then I can drive her to the cottage and visit as much as I like.*

Teddy, Mac and I tried out for a spot in the Under 13 Quads, which is rowing talk for a boat with four sets of oars. Mac and I had never rowed before and it showed. It was heavy-going, much harder than I'd thought it would be, to row in time with three other teammates. Teddy had never rowed before either, but he's a natural oarsman. He's as strong as an ox and got into the right rhythm from the first stroke. It was beautiful to watch. When it started to rain, Mac and I got under the cover of the school boatshed. Teddy was soaking wet when he ran up to meet us.

'I made it, I got into the Quads!' he said, excitedly.

'Congratulations, mate!' Mac and I said, taking it in turns to slap him on the back and shake his hand.

'I'll be rowing in the Easter regatta at the King's School.' Teddy was so proud of himself. We were proud of him too and basked in his glory.

I finally got a letter from Kit. He promised he'd send me one every week, but this was his first:

Dear Joe,

Mr Thompson says I'm the best paperboy he's ever had. I even get tips but he won't let me keep them. He says any money I get belongs to him. No sign of that crook I was telling you about that bashes paperboys and steals their money. I think I must have scared him off.

When Harry put the price of eggs up, Miss Ruxton was real cranky about it. She doesn't like Harry because he gave her a cracked egg once and Harry doesn't like her because she tells him off all the time. Old Billy made him apologise for calling her an old bag.

We got a new boarder. His name is Fred Davis and I think he and Noni are in love. He's not sleeping in your bed anymore – he found a room to let just up the road. Noni has started wearing make-up. She looks different with red lips. Dad reckons she looks like a tart. Fred has black hair and uses lots of oil. He started work for Dad on Saturday. Mum and Dad have been flat out. I'll let you know if Noni and Fred get engaged or anything.

I miss sharing a bedroom with you even though I've got lots more room now. I've moved over onto your bed. I hope you don't mind. It's much better next to the window. I can look out at the old oak tree and watch the moon while I'm lying in bed, just like you used to. We all miss you, even Dad, but he pretends he doesn't. I don't think Noni misses you much since Fred arrived. I caught them kissing on the lounge last night. They had the lights out but there was a full moon so I could see exactly what they were doing. He put his arm around her and they kissed, again and again and again. Their longest kiss lasted about a minute and would have gone longer except Dad came home. Do you think I'm too young to play spin the bottle?

Your loving brother,
Kit
PS Have you kicked Brother Felix in the nuts yet?

The only letter I'd ever written was to Father Christmas and that was years ago. I knew there was no such thing, but I did it for Kit. I even bought a stamp and we posted the letter. What a waste of a stamp that was!

Teddy got called up to the office to see the Monsignor. Mac and I took turns bowling and hitting balls into the cricket net while we waited for him to come back.

'I've got to go home,' he said. 'Dad's had an accident on the farm. He might lose a leg.'

'I'm real sorry, mate,' said Mac.

'How long will you be gone?' I asked.

'Dunno. All depends. With Dad out of action, Mum can't afford to pay anyone else. It's up to me to run the farm, being the only son and all.'

Mac and I looked at each other like a couple of stunned mullets. I couldn't imagine me going home to take over Dad's illegal bookmaking business, and I don't think Mac would've been up to running a bank – not just yet anyway.

Mac and I bowled cricket balls for Teddy to hit into the net. When we went back to the dorm to help him pack, I looked at our three beds all in a row. *We won't be the Three Bears anymore,* I thought. As he finished packing his bag, I looked at the empty bedside table. *I'll miss that photo of him on his horse, and the wooden box he made with a snakeskin inside that was shed by a death adder.*

'You're both welcome to come and visit me on the farm anytime. Maybe even lend a hand.'

'You bet!' I said.

'No worries,' said Mac.

Teddy obviously had more confidence in our abilities than we did. Mac and I are a couple of city boys whose milk is delivered in bottles and whose mums buy meat from the butcher. We don't need to milk cows or slaughter them to survive.

Teddy went home on the train to Queensland by himself. He'll miss rowing in the Under 13 Quads at the Easter regatta. They haven't got a hope in hell of winning without him. I'll miss Papa bear. At least I've still got Mac.

EASTER
CHAPTER 18

I was the first one up as I was keen to get an early start. I got through the morning drill in record time, and then started packing my case.

'What are you doing?' Mac asked.

'Getting ready.'

'You going somewhere?' Mac's not normally dim. He's by far the smartest in the class.

'Timbuktu! Where do you think?' I locked my case and sat on the bed all ready to go.

'You going home?'

'Aren't you?'

'Nobody's allowed to go home at Easter. Rule 124 – everybody knows that.'

I felt like he'd just punched me hard in the guts, winding me. I couldn't breathe. So there really was a rule 124! I thought it was only a joke.

Mum sent me some homemade chocolates for Easter – they arrived that morning. She must've known about rule 124. Mac and I got stuck into the chocolates after lunch and ate the lot. They were too good to bribe the prefects with.

Because I was still on suspension from altar boy duty, I wasn't allowed to serve in the chapel over Easter, which suited me fine. That meant I'd miss out on two Stations of the Cross and a mass on Good Friday, a mass on Easter Saturday and two masses on Easter Sunday. I'd still be there, though, for all the Easter services – rule 129.

Mac woke up early on Good Friday morning with a bad stomach ache. He was doubled over in pain, and thought it might have been the chocolates.

'Are you alright, mate?' I asked.

'I think I'm going to vomit!' And he did – all over the dorm floor. He rolled onto the floor, holding his stomach. It was the first time I'd seen him cry.

Brother Sebastian came in, ringing the wake-up bell, and then stopped dead in his tracks with a look of disgust. 'Whoever made this mess, clean it up!'

'Mac's real sick, sir. Can you please help him?' I pleaded.

Brother Sebastian lifted Mac up off the floor and onto the bed.

'Where does it hurt?' he asked.

'My stomach – it's killing me!'

'Can you walk?'

'No!'

'That's alright, I'm going to carry you to the infirmary. Ready?' Brother Sebastian was also the rugby coach. He lifted Mac up in one go and headed to the infirmary. I followed them every step of the way. We got him there just in the nick of time. Sister Monica suspected appendicitis and called for an ambulance straight away. The thirty minutes it took for the ambulance to arrive seemed like hours.

Mac was operated on soon after he got to Sydney Hospital. Brother Sebastian told us there were complications – Mac's appendix had ruptured. It was touch and go for a while but Brother Sebastian assured me that Mac was going to pull through. Trouble was – he'd be in hospital for another month, maybe longer.

I looked at the empty beds on either side of me. *The Three Bears is just a stupid fairytale anyway,* I thought. *I hate Easter and I hate St Bart's! I'm running away for good this time – to Uncle George's – no-one will find me there.*

The Brothers had been watching me like hawks after my last escape, but everyone was so busy over Easter that they dropped their guard, and just like the first time, I walked out the gate and down the road to the wharf. Nobody saw me or tried to stop me.

But the wharf gate was closed and there was a sign tied to it: 'Due to ferry maintenance, there will be no ferries running over Easter.'

I kicked the gate with all my might and then looked out over the grey, still water. I could see the top of the Harbour Bridge in the distance. Sitting down on the grass, I watched as some seagulls landed, hopping closer and closer to me, waiting for some morsels. They were out of luck and so was I. After picking up a handful of grass and throwing it at them, I walked miserably back up the hill to school. No-one had even missed me.

Nothing's going to stop me from going home next month for the school holidays, I thought. Some of the country boys would have to stay at school because it takes too long for them to do the round trip. By the time they'd get home, they'd have to come back again. I started marking off every day until the holidays in the back of my Arithmetic book.

THE LAST
STRAW

B rother Sebastian left with the senior rugby teams, the First and Second XV, for a tour of boys' boarding schools in country New South Wales. They were playing for the Macquarie Shield, which Brother Sebastian vowed to bring back to St Bart's and hang in the Great Hall. We formed a guard of honour along both sides of the main school driveway, cheering them on their way. As I waved goodbye to Brother Sebastian,

I wondered who'd be replacing him as junior dorm master for the next two weeks.

I was running again – not away from St Bart's just yet – but on the athletics track. With the plaster on my right arm long gone, I could swing it as good as my left, and I felt free as a bird. I was the 'most improved' at athletics training two weeks in a row: first in the Under 13s fifty-yard sprint, and first in the hundred yards. My wins scored me a place on the junior relay team for my house, Mawson, named after Douglas Mawson, the Antarctic explorer. The Athletics Carnival would be on soon, and if I won my races, I'd be representing St Bart's at the big interschool athletics carnival in July. I didn't own a pair of spikes – I prefer to run barefoot – it suits my style.

That day was a good one, better than most: sending off the rugby teams, winning all my races at athletics training and roast lamb, a rare treat, for dinner. Not as good as Mum's, but it still tasted great. I had no kitchen duty and no homework except for reading *Great Expectations* for English.

After supper, it was time for bed. Kneeling down

to say my prayers, I looked at Mac and Teddy's empty beds and felt very alone. I prayed to God that my mates would come back soon. 'In the name of the Father, Son and Holy Ghost, Amen.' Then I jumped into bed.

'Lights out in one minute.' The voice was unmistakable. *Of all the Brothers at St Bart's they could've chosen, they had to pick him!*

When Brother Felix came and sat on my bed, I was alarmed but not scared. 'Your suspension finishes at midnight tonight,' he said. 'I expect you to be at altar practice tomorrow afternoon.'

'Yes, sir.'

He squeezed my shoulder. 'You've always been my favourite, Joe.' I couldn't believe that Brother Felix had actually called me 'Joe' and that I was his favourite! 'I didn't tell you before because I didn't want the other boys to be envious. As you know, envy is one of the seven deadly sins.'

When he got up and turned off the lights, I couldn't see him anymore. Then I heard footsteps and felt someone sit on my bed.

'Shhh,' he said softly, as he stroked my face.

I couldn't believe that Brother Felix was actually stroking my face! I felt him put his other hand under the bed covers. His fingers were near my belly button. For a split second, I felt him touch me where he shouldn't.

Something snapped. I punched him in the face with all my might. We both cried out in pain. I shook my hand – it was killing me. I rubbed my eyes with my other hand – there was something warm and sticky on my face. When one of the boys turned on the lights, I saw blood everywhere.

'You little bastard, I think you've broken my nose!' Brother Felix held a handkerchief to his nose and then hurried out of the dorm. Everyone clapped and cheered. I was shaking. If Brother Felix could've seen me through all the blood that was on his face, I think he would have throttled me.

———

Brother Damian, the senior boarding master, ran in and dragged me out of bed. 'Come with me to the office. Back to sleep, the rest of you.'

When I told Monsignor Reynolds and Brother Damian what had happened, they wouldn't believe me. The Monsignor said I was telling lies to get out of trouble and that if I didn't repent my sins and change my evil ways, I'd go to hell. I felt like I was already there.

'I could contact the police and have you charged with assault,' he explained, 'but that is not the way we address problems like yourself at St Bartholomew's. If word gets out, respectable parents might start taking their boys out of the school. The reputation of this college is paramount.'

For breaking Brother Felix's nose and telling 'defamatory lies' about him, I was put into one of the isolation rooms where 'in solitude, you can reflect on your hideous deeds and pray to God for forgiveness.' I kicked the walls of the isolation room and pulled my bed apart, shouting out every swear word that I knew. The room was the size of a confessional or large dunny, with a small window at the top that was too high to reach, even when I stood on the upturned bed.

As soon as my parents could be contacted and arrangements made, I was being sent to St Mary's

Farm School, a reformatory on the south coast run by some nuns. I hoped and prayed that Mum and Dad would refuse to go along with their plan and that I could go home.

For three nights, I was kept in the isolation room under the watchful eye of Brother Damian, who brought me breakfast, lunch and dinner on a tray. I was only allowed out to go to the dunny, and so was forbidden to take part in any school activities, which, he told me, included the Liturgy on the last day of term as well as the long-table dinner hosted by the senior boys for staff, parents (except mine) and special guests. I think he expected me to be upset or, at the very least, disappointed about what I was missing out on. *He hasn't got a clue!* I thought. But when he told me that my parents had agreed to the reformatory and that I wouldn't even be going home for the holidays, I flew into a rage, kicking the walls and pulling my bed apart again. I managed to break the window with a broken bed leg, and when the glass fell on my head, I swore like a trooper. The threat of hell and damnation had no effect on my rage.

Monsignor Reynolds had to make another home visit because as far as he knew Mum and Dad didn't have a telephone. One of Dad's mates had installed an illegal line for us so that some of the punters could call their bets in. Dad had bought the telephone cheap from another mate at the pub. We have an unlisted number that only a select group of people know about.

Brother Damian was smirking when he told me that St Mary's was at the foot of a mountain, ten miles to the nearest railway station. 'Running away won't be possible. Through manual labour, prayer and sacrifice, you will learn humility, respect and responsibility.'

I spent my last night at St Bart's with Brother Damian's words and crooked, yellow teeth going around and around in my head.

SOUTH TO ST MARY'S

CHAPTER 20

Dad and I boarded the South Coast train at Central Station, stopping all stations to Bomaderry. The furthest I'd ever been on a train was out to Uncle George's chook farm in Rooty Hill to pick up eggs. I'd never left Sydney, never been away anywhere on a holiday. Mac has been to Amsterdam, the capital of Holland. He sailed with his family on a ship to Batavia in the Dutch East Indies and then by aeroplane to Amsterdam – it's the longest air route in the world.

The train rattled its way through the city, hissing steam and blowing clouds of smoke that wafted through the window and stung my throat. Looking out the window at all the houses, factories and shops crowded together, I thought they seemed out of place, as if they belonged somewhere else, like in England, which I'd read about in *Great Expectations*. On the outskirts of the city, I saw shacks and humpies where poor people lived on the sand dunes of Botany Bay, not far from where Captain Cook had landed in 1770.

Things were going from bad to worse, not the way I'd planned at all. I'd always felt like a winner, and not just on the athletics track or cricket pitch, or when I'd won the Glebe Billycart Derby. I found opportunities to make money, to make something of my life. I'd felt that the world really was my oyster. Now I felt like all I had left were the stinking empty oyster shells. Looking on the bright side, there was only one way left for me to go, and that was up.

Dad fell asleep with his head resting on the back of the train seat. He started snoring but with the noise the train made, I don't think anyone else noticed. Sticking my hand out the window, I touched the leaves of a gum tree that brushed past, and then bumped my head on the glass trying to spot koalas up in the trees that were growing all along the track. Smoke and cinders from the engine blew in my face, stinging my eyes. I kept blinking to try and stop the burning feeling.

When we entered a long dark tunnel, I closed my eyes and imagined that I was flying in a plane to Amsterdam with Mac and Teddy. There was no-one in the cockpit so we sat down and took over the controls, flying the plane like we'd done it a hundred times before. Suddenly the cockpit started to fill with smoke and a bright light was shining in my eyes, almost blinding me. When I opened my eyes, I was relieved to see that I was on the train, but disappointed to be sitting next to Dad, who was still snoring.

As we came out of the tunnel into daylight again,

the train swept around a big bend, and then everything went blue. The train was crossing a high bridge over a creek, and the blue was the Pacific Ocean that seemed to go on forever. When I squinted, I could just make out a ship on the horizon. It looked so small it must've been miles away. I wanted to be on that ship, sailing to Batavia, just like Mac had done.

I used to go fishing in Botany Bay with Dad and his mate, Stan. We'd go out in Stan's dinghy, and the fish would almost jump into the boat. We never came back empty-handed. There was always plenty of bream, flathead and trevally to take home to cook for dinner and sell to the neighbours.

The train rattled on past steep cliffs on one side and beaches, fishing boats and a lighthouse on the other. I dozed off with the rocking of the train and dreamt that the reformatory was on a headland with its own lighthouse, and I was lost at sea in a small boat. I could see the light from the lighthouse, but no matter how hard I paddled, I couldn't get any closer to it. Then a loud whistle woke me up, and I saw a sign flash past again and again: 'Wollongong'.

We followed the coastline south, past the smoking chimney stacks and new steelworks at Port Kembla, and then headed inland through farmlands, away from a big lake and towards the mountains. As the train pulled into Dapto Station, I woke Dad up.

'Is this our stop?' I asked.

'No, next one.' Those were the first words he'd spoken to me the whole way from Central Station. 'Why did you do it, Joe?' he asked, clenching his fist. 'Why did you punch that Brother in the face?'

'I don't know, I just did.' How could I tell my father that another man, an ordained Brother, had touched me where he shouldn't? Maybe I'd overreacted, maybe it was an accident, but every instinct in my body told me no, that wasn't it at all. I don't regret what I did. *That bastard got what he deserved.*

Dad and I were the only people to get off the train at Yallah. It was Sunday morning so I figured everyone must be at Church. A man in overalls was waiting outside the station, standing alongside two horses and a cart, and smoking a pipe.

'Are ya the Rileys?' he asked.

'I'm Arthur Riley and this is my son, Joe.'

'I'm Henry Lucas — caretaker, driver, butcher, farmer an' jack-o'-all-trades at St Mary's. I'll look after ya son from 'ere. School's 'bout ten miles up the road. The next train back to Sydney should be 'ere soon.'

Dad shook my hand. 'Don't go getting up to any mischief.'

'I won't.' I didn't say goodbye because I was still angry with him for sending me away. I climbed up onto the seat next to Henry.

'G'day, Joe,' he said. Henry had one of those friendly sounding voices. As soon as we turned around on the gravel roadway, the horses started trotting and Dad was nowhere in sight.

'They know their own way home,' Henry said. 'I'm just 'ere to hold the reins. They hafta get a bit o' speed so we can make it up that hill. Don't worry, they know when to slow down.'

We rode over one hill, then another and another. I couldn't see for the dust, which started working its way into my eyes, nose and mouth, even my ears. *Bloody hell!* I thought.

'Are we nearly there?' I asked. Henry didn't seem to hear me over the noise of the hooves crashing on the dirt roadway, so I shouted, 'Are we nearly there?'

'Ya don't hafta shout, I heard ya the first time! Ya city boys hafta learn to be patient, give people time to answer.' I could barely see Henry through all the dust that was flying up. 'Couple more miles,' he shouted.

Eventually, we turned left through some gates onto a narrow dirt track, and then a sign flashed past.

'Is this it?' I asked.

'Yep, St Mary's Farm School alright. We call it the Farm.'

The horses picked up speed and started to canter, brushing past overhanging bush on both sides of the track, yellow wattle spraying all over us like confetti. We pulled up outside a large timber house with a verandah that looked like it went all the way around. I had grit in my eyes and a mouthful of dirt that I spat out as soon as I jumped down from the cart. There was a small kangaroo grazing a few yards away. I'd never seen a live kangaroo before, just dead ones alongside the train tracks near Uncle George's chook farm. Looking up, I saw the sun shining above a tree-covered mountain that was so big it cast a shadow over the house. It was dark and mysterious, almost god-like, looming over everything. When I looked around to find the kangaroo, it was gone.

THE FARM
CHAPTER 21

A tall nun wearing a long brown habit and a large set of rosary beads around her waist was striding towards me with her arm outstretched, ready to shake my hand. 'You must be Joseph Riley. Welcome to the Farm. I'm Sister Agnes, the School Principal.'

The only nun I'd ever met before was Sister Monica, the nurse at St Bart's. I'm not exactly sure she was a nun, but she was an angel sent from heaven. Sister Agnes doesn't look like an angel – she walks and talks more like a man. I could feel the bones in my hand crunch as we shook hands.

'Unfortunately you missed Mass this morning – it's the highlight of our week. Father Brian comes out from Dapto early every Sunday morning to hear confession and celebrate Mass with us.' She put her hands together and closed her eyes. I wasn't sure if she was thinking hard about something or praying. Half a minute later she opened her eyes and smiled, rubbing her hands together. 'I'll show you the classroom on our way to your cabin. You'll need to get changed into some work clothes.'

I followed her along the verandah around to the side of the house, and then through some open doors.

'This is our classroom – on Sundays it serves as a chapel.'

There were five rows of desks facing a blackboard with a big crucifix and pull-down charts at the top. In one corner there was a lectern, and in the other, a statue of Our Lady surrounded by vases of fresh flowers. The room was very neat and didn't look like it had been used very often.

We walked around to the back of the house and looked through the window at the big kitchen, then we stopped to admire a long table and four benches on the verandah.

'Henry made all of these from trees that had fallen down on our property,' she said, running her fingers along the grain of the smooth wood. 'Most of your meals will be served here. And over there's the barn where you'll go for milking duty twice a day.' She pointed to a huge tin shed that was much bigger than the house.

There was a strong smell of fresh cow manure in the air, and I could hear cows mooing not too far away. I pinched myself to make sure I wasn't dreaming.

We started walking towards two cabins that were opposite the barn and looked like shacks with crooked verandahs out the front.

'There are sixteen boys in each cabin, and you'll be sleeping in this one.' she said, as we stepped onto a creaking verandah, crowded with broken beds, two buckets and a large wooden box. Inside, the cabin was set out like a dorm with eight beds on either side.

'This is your bed,' she said, pointing to the fourth bed along on the wall closest to the barn.

I lifted my case onto the rusty metal-framed bed with no bedspread, just a grey woollen army blanket tucked in with a grey sheet.

'The showers are outside in the shed and the toilet is down the back near the flame trees. These are your work clothes to change into. You can put your case under the bed – you won't be needing it for a while.' She clapped her hands together – they were thick and fleshy like a man's and her fingernails were black with dirt. 'I'll wait for you outside on the verandah.'

The cabin wasn't quite what I'd expected – some of the panes of glass in the windows were broken, and there were bars on the outside and no curtains on the inside. *My home away from home*, I thought. Above the doorway was another big crucifix, while a cracked and faded painting of Our Lady holding baby Jesus looked down on me from the cabin wall.

It felt good to take off my St Bart's uniform and stow it away under the bed. It was hard to believe that earlier that day, I was still locked in an isolation room at St Bart's wearing a woollen blazer, tie and black leather school shoes; and then five hours later I was at a reformatory in the country putting on overalls and going barefoot. *Teddy would be proud of me*, I thought, as I walked out onto the verandah.

'Find a pair of gumboots that fit,' Sister Agnes said, pointing to the wooden box and then closing her eyes. While I rummaged through the box of gumboots, she rubbed her rosary beads and prayed.

I tried on one boot after another until I found a matching pair that I could walk in without falling over. They all seemed to be either large or extra-large.

I stood there waiting for Sister Agnes to stop praying and open her eyes. She looked so peaceful – I didn't want to disturb her.

'The boys are working down in the vegetable garden,' she said, suddenly looking straight at me. 'Go over the first cattle stop, past the barn and the cattle and sheep paddocks, then over the second cattle stop. Sister Cornelius will be waiting for you.'

Sister Agnes walked back to the house, leaving me to find my own way. I had no idea what a cattle stop was and I wasn't sure that I deserved her trust at this early stage of the game.

On my way to the barn, I crossed a small bridge built into the track with wide gaps between the timber slats. *Must be a cattle stop,* I thought, *because it'd be impossible for cows to get across without falling through the gaps.*

Walking past paddocks with cattle and sheep grazing, I felt a sense of freedom that I hadn't felt in a long time. I couldn't believe that this was my punishment for punching Brother Felix in the face and breaking his nose. It was heaven compared to the isolation room at St Bart's.

I wasn't watching where I was going and tripped over what must have been the second cattle stop, getting splinters in my hand. I got up and looked around but couldn't see anyone.

Further along on my right was an orchard with apple, orange, lemon and other fruit trees. There were only a handful of apples left high up in the trees but lots of oranges and lemons ready for picking.

As I stopped to pull the splinters out of my hand, I watched the sun sink behind the mountain, which was so close I felt that I could reach out and touch it. The pink sky was fading to grey and a cold wind was blowing; it was the start of winter.

CABBAGES AND CAULIFLOWERS

CHAPTER 22

'Hello, Joe – over here!' a nun wearing a brown habit, dirty white apron, gumboots and swinging a stick called out. She was standing on a mound of dirt surrounded by a group of boys who seemed more interested in watching me than doing any work. Hurrying towards me, she wiped her dirty hands on her apron then held out a hand for me to shake. 'I'm Sister Cornelius, your English, Science and Gardening teacher. Grab a hoe and start digging. We need to get this manure turned over and mixed in ready for spring. Get cracking – it'll be dark soon.' She didn't look big enough or old enough to be a nun, and the stick she was holding was almost as tall as she was. There were at least twenty boys in the veggie garden wearing overalls and gumboots just like mine, only dirtier. I looked at the tools they were using and picked up one like theirs.

'That hoe's no good, mate. The head keeps flyin' off,' a small boy next to me said.

'No talking, Pete. You know the drill,' said Sister Cornelius. I took Pete's advice and picked up a different hoe.

It felt good digging in the dirt. The manure was all dried out and didn't smell at all. I swung the hoe higher and higher until I got into a rhythm. The last garden tool I remembered using was a shovel to dig a hole in the backyard to bury our old cat, Sammy.

'Well done, boys!' Sister Cornelius called out. 'Time to pack up the tools and get these cabbages and cauliflowers to the kitchen.'

We piled up the cabbages and cauliflowers as high

as we could in the wheelbarrow and then carried the rest. They were so big we could only carry two each.

'Cabbage makes me fart,' Pete said, juggling his two cabbages.

'Me too,' I said, and we both laughed.

'Watch this!' he said, throwing a cabbage in the air and kicking it three times before catching it. When I tried to do the same, my cabbage split open. I quickly picked up the two halves before Sister Cornelius noticed.

We carried them to the kitchen, waiting outside on the verandah. It was the first time that I'd met Mrs Lucas – the cook, housekeeper and Henry's wife. She isn't as friendly as Henry, and is about twice his size.

'Where am I s'posed to put all those?' she said, throwing her arms up in the air. 'Ya may as well leave 'em in the wheelbarra an' put the rest on the table. At this rate, we'll be eatin' cabbages an' cauliflowers till the cows come home.'

We did our best to balance them on the long table but as soon as we walked away, some of the cabbages rolled off. Pete and I kept going; it wasn't our problem anymore.

While two boys took it in turns to pump water from a forty-four gallon drum, the rest of us lined up, washing our hands in the outside washbasin that looked more like a cattle trough. The water in the trough was a dark grey by the time it was my turn to wash. Showers are only every second day so I'd have to wait another day for that privilege.

I was one of the boys on wood duty, so I carried armfuls of chopped wood into the kitchen and stacked them next to the fireplace for Mrs Lucas.

A huge kettle and two enormous pots were hanging from chains over the blazing fire. It was much warmer in the kitchen than outside on the verandah where I then sat down with the rest of the boys, shivering and waiting for dinner to be served. The nuns sat inside around the kitchen table with Henry and Mrs Lucas to eat their dinner.

We had cabbage and cauliflower soup that night, which tasted better than it sounds. The hot freshly baked bread wasn't half bad either. Mrs Lucas might be an old grump, but she knows how to cook.

After the table was cleared and the dishes washed,

wiped and put away, I needed to go to the dunny. Looking around out the back in the dark, I couldn't see anything.

'Where's the dunny?' I asked Pete.

He put up his hand to get the attention of Sister Cornelius. 'Sister, can I show Joe where the dunny is?'

'You know the rules, Pete – it's one at a time. Joe, you just need to go down the track past the cabins until you get to the flame trees then turn right. You can't miss it.'

With only a kerosene lantern to light my way, I followed the dirt track, my gum boots flicking up stones as I walked. I watched the light from my lantern reflecting back at me from the cabin windows. A family of kookaburras started laughing in the nearby flame trees, their laughter echoing off the mountain that was hidden in the darkness. Crickets were chirping all around, and I could feel eyes watching me the whole time. I managed to find the dunny, which, at first, looked like any other dunny back home. The timber was held together with a few rusty nails and the door was hanging off. I heard a buzzing sound before I smelt the stench. Inside, the toilet was just a hole in the ground, a bit like Uncle George's but more disgusting and covered with the biggest flies I'd ever seen.

I wandered over to the flame trees and peed there instead, deciding that if I drank and ate less, I wouldn't have to go to the toilet as often, and that whenever I got the chance, I'd just go somewhere in the bush. I remembered Walter, an Aboriginal boy at Glebe Public School, telling me that soft leaves and grass are just as good, if not better than newspaper for wiping your bum. I was keen to put it to the test.

After dinner, Sister Cornelius and Sister Ambrose (who's young like Sister Cornelius but much bigger) took it in turns to tell us Bible stories and parables around the campfire that was blazing on the far side of the cabins. It was magical listening to their soft Irish voices, watching the flames rising out of the burning logs. I lost myself in the stories about Cain and Abel, Abraham and the rest of the family. I can't believe that Cain killed his own brother!

It was a dark, starry night without any moon, and pitch black when it was time to go to bed.

A kerosene lamp was flickering on the verandah of the cabin and I could see two buckets, one at either end – our night toilets – so that we didn't have to find our way out the back in the dark.

That first night, I kept warm by breathing and farting under my two thin blankets. Judging by the noises and smells coming from the other beds, we were all doing the same thing. Must have been the cabbage and cauliflower soup we had for dinner.

GETTING THE HANG OF IT
CHAPTER 23

'Wake up, mate, yer on bucket duty.'

Pulling my overalls up over the shirt I'd slept in, I followed a broad-shouldered boy with a deep voice I'd recognised from the day before, out onto the verandah.

'Pick up that bucket, I'll get this one,' he said. 'There's a trench down near the creek where we empty 'em.'

As soon as I picked up the bucket and started

walking, yellow pee and brown turds splashed onto my overalls and bare feet. Everyone laughed, and some boys whistled. They were all watching, waiting for the show, and I didn't disappoint.

'G'day, I'm Lance, ya team foreman. Congratulations, yer officially a Farm boy,' he said, smirking. One of his front teeth was missing and the other one was black. I shook hands with him, even though I felt like punching his head in. Lance put a pole through the handle of my bucket. 'Grab the other end – it takes two to empty a night bucket.'

We walked along the dirt track, down past the orchard and veggie garden, emptying the first bucket into a trench, not too far from a creek that flowed around the base of the mountain. 'Alright then,' Lance said, 'let's get the other one. I'll race ya.' He got a head start but I was faster – I ran like the wind. By the time I jumped onto the verandah, Lance was still coming past the barn. When all the boys cheered, I raised the pole in the air, waving it around like a flag.

'Smart arse,' Lance said, as we picked up the second bucket.

The barn is also the milking shed. Every morning and afternoon, we're on rosters to herd the cows into the shed, wash their teats ready for milking, milk them by hand, collect the milk buckets for separating or to go straight to the kitchen, use a separator to take the cream out, wash up everything, and then herd the cows back into their paddock.

Pete showed me how to use the separator the first time I was on milking duty. As I turned the handle, he poured in bucket after bucket of fresh, warm milk, which spun around and around. The heavier milk moved towards the walls of the separator, while the lighter cream stayed in the middle. Milk started pouring out the bottom spout into one bucket while cream ran out the top spout into another. As each bucket of milk filled up, Pete swapped it for an empty one.

We took the buckets of separated milk to the kitchen for breakfast, as well as half a bucket of cream for Mrs Lucas to churn into butter.

It'd be so much easier to just buy the milk and butter,

I thought. By the time we cleaned the separator, buckets and ladles, I was starving.

Mrs Lucas had two large pots of bubbling porridge ready to serve. My mouth was watering as we said grace. There was no sugar, just honey from the beehives, which tastes even better. I poured milk and honey all over my porridge, mixing it in. Delicious! No sooner had Mrs Lucas put the bread and butter on the table than it was all gone. Henry supervised the boys on tea duty who poured thirty-two cups of hot tea, leaving room in the cups for lots of fresh milk and honey. Yum! I was on clearing up duty so I got to lick one of the ladles. I could've eaten a whole potful of porridge, I was so hungry. The porridge was much better than the slop we used to get at St Bart's.

Sister Agnes, Sister Cornelius and Sister Ambrose (or the Three Sisters as we call them) eat breakfast by themselves then join us when the tea is poured. Sister Agnes, the Principal, is always bright and cheery in the morning, but as the day wears on, she gets crankier and crankier until by late afternoon – watch out! 'Good morning, boys. We are going to be blessed with another beautiful day,' she says every morning – rain, hail or shine; only the roster changes.

'About the roster for this morning: Lance, Pete, Charlie and Joe are on water duty. You'll need to water the vegetable garden and fill up the animal troughs, kitchen basins and shower drums – it's shower day. Trevor, Ray, Douglas and Tom are on wood duty. Now that the weather's turned cold, we need a lot more wood chopped and split. Make sure you put all of the unseasoned wood in the barn, and only stack up the older, dried-out logs on the verandah.'

And so the roster goes on until each of the eight work teams has been given their list of chores, which can also include: weeding, pruning and picking fruit and veggies in the orchard and veggie garden; clearing scrub, roots, rocks and weeds from a new paddock to get ready for ploughing; cleaning out the barn and chook pen; looking after the stock; digging up charcoal and making new pits; planting seeds, seedlings and trees; building and repairing fences; and collecting honey from the beehives (under Henry's watchful eye).

Water duty is a real chore. That day, I made twenty-seven trips, filling up and carting buckets of water from the creek to water the veggies, then filling up the animal and kitchen troughs, and the killer forty-four gallon shower drums.

It took our team more than three hours, two swims and four water fights to do water duty. We'd tried to fire up the old pump to pump water from the creek to the veggie garden, but all it did was cough black soot over us. On our last trip back down to the creek to fill up the buckets, Pete was the first one to take off his overalls and jump in the water. It was our second swim of the day.

'Is it still cold?' I called out, undoing my overalls.

'Find out for yaself!' Lance said, pushing me into the creek. It wasn't cold, it was freezing.

'Bastard!' I yelled, throwing my wet overalls at him, and then splashing him with as much water as I could before swimming away towards Pete. I caught up with him in the middle of the creek. Lance and Charlie stayed on the bank watching us. Neither of them could swim.

'I'm glad I've got a swimmin' partner,' Pete said. 'Not as much fun swimmin' out here by meself. Do ya wanna see a waterfall?'

'You bet!' I swam with Pete further up the creek, through a school of very small fish that were darting about, trying to avoid us. The water was crystal clear but getting too deep to stand up in. Suddenly, something long, thin and snake-like glided past underneath me, going in the other direction. I caught up to Pete and tapped him on the shoulder.

'Did you see that snake?' I asked, treading water.

'It wasn't a snake, it was an eel,' he said, laughing. 'Take a look at that beauty!' Pete pointed up at the mountain and the biggest waterfall I'd ever seen – actually it was the only waterfall I'd ever seen. Water was flowing over a rock ledge, half-way up the mountain, splashing into the creek below. 'Ya wanna swim under it?' he asked.

'You bet!' I shouted, swimming with him under the waterfall to the rock face, then in and out so many times, I lost count. It was a lot of fun, but we couldn't keep it up for too long, we had work to do.

'Ya lazy bludgers, get out o' there!' Lance said, waving his arms about. At least that's what I thought he said – I couldn't actually hear him. He was about fifty yards away, jumping up and down on the creek bank.

Pete and I planned our attack. We swam back and filled up our buckets of water, put our overalls back on and then followed Lance and Charlie to the shower drums. Pete poured his bucket into one of the drums, while I tipped in the water from my first bucket then threw the next one over Lance before running as fast as I could towards the flame trees for lunch. I was a marked man, but it was worth it to get back at Lance.

The Three Sisters were waiting impatiently for us with the rest of the boys under the flame trees. No-one seemed to notice that my overalls were wet.

Lance was fuming when he arrived, and kept giving me the evil eye. I don't know why he was so angry; it was clean creek water that I threw over him, not the muck from the night buckets that went all over me that first morning.

There were loaves of freshly baked bread, a slab of butter and a couple of jars of blackberry jam from

Mrs Lucas's pantry spread out on a rug on the grass. After saying grace and quickly demolishing my two slices, I took the opportunity to lie down and dry off in the noon-day sun.

This is the life, I thought. *Beats Rowing, Rugby and 'Rithmetic at St Bart's any day.*

THE PITS

After lunch we stood up under the flame trees, saying prayers and singing hymns. Sister Agnes has a beautiful voice, but although Sister Cornelius and Sister Ambrose sing with passion, they're always out of time and out of tune – not a good combination. If more boys would've sung properly instead of mumbling, we wouldn't have had to suffer listening to Sister Cornelius and Sister Ambrose sing their hearts out.

As everyone was on charcoal duty that afternoon, we made our way past the orchard, veggie garden and beehives to the charcoal pits. There were piles of dead wood and mounds of dirt in the paddock, but no sign of any charcoal.

Lance handed the shovels to our team. 'There are charcoal pits under all that dirt. We hafta dig out all the charcoal before we can make a new pit. Yer gunna love this, Joe!'

While Lance stood there barking orders, Charlie, Pete and I shovelled dirt from the top of our mound until we hit something made of metal.

'We need to do the rest by hand,' Lance said. 'That tin's razor sharp.' Getting down on our hands and knees, we removed all of the dirt from the overlapping sheets of tin. 'Be real careful liftin' 'em off or ya'll slice ya hands open.'

Under the tin was a large pit filled with lumps of charcoal.

'Joe, go get a dozen hessian bags from Sister Ambrose to pack this lot into,' Lance said, grinning.

What he didn't tell me until I got back was that

Pete and I would be digging up the charcoal and filling the bags while he and Charlie started collecting dead wood for the new pit. This was payback and I wasn't about to argue the toss. It was hard, filthy work and by the time Pete and I'd finished shovelling all of the charcoal into bags, we were black from head to toe.

'What's all this charcoal for anyway?' I asked Pete.

'Fuel for Henry's truck, mostly,' he replied. 'The Three Sisters also need some for their hot-water heater an' the copper in the laundry. Charcoal burns hotter than wood, ya know.'

I'd never heard of trucks that ran on charcoal before and couldn't see them taking off in Sydney.

We wandered down to the creek to have a drink and cool off. The creek was in the shadow of the mountain at that time of the afternoon. It was cold in the shade and the water was icy – refreshing to drink but too cold for a swim. Pete and I sat on the creek bank, listening to the frogs croaking. They were so loud and annoying that I started to get a headache.

'Let's go to the orchard an' pick some fruit,' Pete said, jumping to his feet.

We ran around the orchard, picking as many oranges and grapefruit as we could carry back for afternoon tea. Sister Ambrose used a razor-sharp pocket knife that hangs off her rosary beads to cut the fruit in half. By the time I'd polished off two oranges and a grapefruit, I had juice running down my arms and chin. Pete and I volunteered to take all the skins to the compost heap next to the veggie garden. Nothing is ever wasted at the Farm. There are no garbage bins – what can't be re-used in some way gets burned in the incinerator.

It was time to make a new charcoal pit – the last thing I felt like doing. Charlie and Lance passed dead branches and small logs down to Pete and me, and our job was to make layers with them inside the pit. At least it was easier than shovelling charcoal into bags. When there were enough layers, we grabbed handfuls of twigs and dry leaves to fill up the spaces. The ground around our pit was totally cleared. There wasn't a leaf or blade of grass left in sight – smooth as a cricket pitch.

We all lent a hand to light the fire in our pit. Sister

Ambrose gave us some matches but it wasn't easy getting the wood and leaves alight. There was a lot of smoke but not much flame. When it was finally burning hot, we covered the pit with the sheets of tin then shovelled the dirt back on top.

The pit work isn't over until the bags of charcoal are loaded onto Henry's cart, and more dead wood and branches collected to dry out for the next charcoal duty in a few weeks' time. With everyone pitching in, the charcoal was loaded onto the cart in no time.

'I'll meet you boys back at the barn in half an hour,' Sister Ambrose called out, taking off in the horse-drawn cart.

'The best wood is down by the creek. I'll race ya,' Pete said, taking off and already a few yards in front. He was fast but I soon caught up and could've overtaken him but didn't.

'Over here,' he said, climbing up a river gum that was overhanging the creek bank.

We sat quietly on one of the branches, and watched as Lance and Charlie ran to the water's edge, looking all around. They were almost directly below us.

'Where are they?' Charlie asked.

'I don't trust 'em,' said Lance.

I signalled one, two, three, then we jumped. I landed on Lance's back, while Pete jumped on Charlie, the four of us wrestling on the creek bank.

'Ya little bastard!' Lance shouted. He rolled me over and then grabbed my feet in his large man hands, dragging me face down into the creek. I tried to throw my body around to break free but couldn't. 'Time to teach ya a lesson!' he said, as I thrashed about, swallowing water.

'Let him go, he'll drown!' Pete shouted. As soon as Lance let go of my feet, I rolled over and saw Pete on Lance's back – but not for long. Lance swung around and threw him off into the water.

'That'll teach both o' yer who's boss 'round here!' Lance stormed off back to the pits.

'He's a nut case,' said Pete. I was busy coughing water out of my lungs, but couldn't have agreed more.

'Ya should see him on a bad day,' Charlie said, offering me his hand to get up out of the water. Walking along the creek bank, we picked up as many dead branches and small logs as we could carry to the pits. When we got back, Lance wasn't there; nobody was.

I was tired and hungry – we all were, and still had milking duty to do. On the way to the barn, I looked at the sheep in the paddock and the chooks in the pen in a new light. They were no longer woolly lambs and clucking chooks, but mouth-watering Sunday roast dinners.

With the milking and separating done and the cows herded back into the paddock, it was all hands on deck to get the showers ready. There were two cold-water drums and a hot one outside the shower shed. One team was on pump duty with the cold drums, while another kept the fire going under the hot drum and pumped warm water into the shed.

The rest of us took it in turns to strip off and shower. There are only three shower heads in the shed and no taps. Although cold water is always being pumped, it only comes out in fits and bursts. Every ten seconds, warm water is pumped through as well, but only enough to make it bearable. There's just enough water to work up a lather with the one bar of soap we have to share, but at least the showers aren't freezing cold like at St Bart's. I had to scrub my skin with a brush to get all the black soot and dirt off, and was red raw by the time I'd finished. I looked like a skinned rabbit.

Henry brought jars of sticky sap that had been squeezed from a cactus plant for us to rub onto our skin to soothe and calm it down. It worked a treat.

MATES

It didn't take long for me to settle into the daily routines of the Farm. Although every part of my body was aching, I was starting to enjoy the hard, physical work. I'd also made some friends.

Pete and Charlie are my new best mates. Forget about the Three Bears – that's kid's stuff. The rules have changed and I was playing with the big boys now. There are bullies like Lance and outsiders like Charlie and Pete – the boys that no-one ever wants to play with in the playground. It's different at the Farm, you can't be too picky about who your friends are.

Charlie's my second-best mate. He's big for his age, a bit slow but not stupid. He hadn't said more than two words to me until the incident at the creek. Once he started talking, though, it was hard to stop him: 'Lived with me grandparents since I was five. Mum an' Dad just up an' left one day to go fruit pickin' an' never came home. "Better off without 'em," is what Gran an' Grandad said.

'After a few years, I started gettin' into trouble, breakin' into people's homes; stole money an' liquor mostly. I got caught one too many times. Me grandparents, bein' the good Catholics they are, turned to the parish priest rather than the police. That priest had it in for me from the very first time I broke into his presbytery. I only stole a few coins – he had a whole jarful anyway. I never cleaned anyone out, always left somethin' behind. Times are hard – it's the Depression, ya know.

'If I got thirsty on the job, I'd take a few swigs o' whatever was lyin' aroun' – rum, brandy, sherry, beer – I tried 'em all. It wasn't long before I got a taste for liquor, so I started stealin' that too. Not sure if it was the money or the liquor that bastard priest was more worried about. I was too drunk to understand what he was tryin' to tell me.'

Apart from beer, the only liquor I'd had in my life was a few sips of altar wine that Harry gave me when Father Dennis wasn't watching. It looked like blood and tasted like vinegar – I nearly choked on it. Not my thing at all.

Pete's been my best mate since my first day at the Farm. He looks just like my little brother, Kit, except he has straight brown hair. They have the same blue eyes and crooked smile, and climb trees like monkeys – they could be a trapeze act in a circus. If Pete wasn't two years older, they could pass for twins.

Unlike Charlie, Pete isn't the one with the drinking problem in his family – it's his stepdad. Pete hates his stepdad and, by the sound of things, the feeling is mutual. Pete has two half-sisters who are much younger than him.

'If I go anywhere near Elsie an' Dot, I get a beltin' even if I'm just playin' games with 'em. I cop the blame for everythin',' he said. There are still yellow and green bruises on Pete's small, skinny body from the last belting his stepdad gave him.

'What does your mum do when your dad belts you?' I asked. I can relate to beltings, having had a few myself.

'He's not me dad – me real dad's dead. Mum's got a photo of Dad in his army uniform. Half Chinese he was. His father came out here from China lookin' for gold, an' then he met me gran an' married her. I wish me Dad was still alive – he'd stick up for me. When me stepdad belts me, Mum just keeps doin' whatever she's doin' an' minds her own business, otherwise he lays into her. Sometimes she even takes his side. Makes me sick. She never sticks up for me, says I'm just like me father. I'm glad I'm not like me stepdad – I hate him.' Pete gets really angry every time he talks about his stepdad.

'Why were you sent here?' I asked. It didn't make any sense.

'Tried to top meself. The doctor said I was a danger to meself an' me family. He's the one sent me here – pays me board as well.'

It had never occurred to me that you'd have to pay

money to stay at the Farm. Times were much tougher than I'd thought.

Listening to Pete's story, I felt like a wimp. I had nothing to complain about — well maybe not nothing, just nowhere near as much as Pete. I was paying for my crime, which is more than I could say for Brother Felix. If I hadn't punched him in the face, he would've got off scot-free. But Pete didn't do anything wrong. It's not fair! Mum says, 'There's always somebody worse off than yourself.' Pete's worse off than most.

Lance isn't a mate, but since he's the foreman of our work team, I've got to know him pretty well, and I don't like him. Sometimes, he gets this evil look in his eyes — it sends shivers down my spine. He was bragging about how he got into a fight in the city once, and a boy pulled a knife on him. When he tried to defend himself, Lance reckoned he stabbed the boy in the chest with his own knife. I have my doubts. Lance tells more lies than I do. I try my best to give him a wide berth but he brings out the worst in me.

The work's hard and the days are long but I've never been so fit and strong. I'm learning heaps of things:

how to chop and split wood, dig holes with a stick, milk cows and separate the cream, make charcoal pits, collect honey from beehives, plough fields and grow veggies; and how to work so hard that I forget about St Bart's, my best friend Harry, the neighbours back home, Father Dennis and sometimes even my family.

LESSONS

CHAPTER 26

It's hard getting up before the sun does on cold winter mornings. I prefer to do the milking rather than the separating. A cow's warm udder and teats full of milk take the chill out of my hands on a cold morning. Before my first bucket is full, I'm warm all over.

Whether we feel like it or not, we have to milk the cows and do the separating every morning and afternoon – rain, hail or shine.

I'd been at the Farm for over two weeks before it rained enough to have a lesson in the classroom.

All our lessons, except Science, take place when it's too wet or windy to work outside. Sister Agnes says it all evens out in the end, and she should know, she's the Arithmetic teacher.

My first lesson in the classroom was Arithmetic with Sister Agnes, who also teaches Religion, Music and Latin. I've learnt about more weights and measures than I ever knew existed. I'd thought the smallest weight possible was an ounce, but it's not. There are 256 drachms in an ounce and 7000 grains in a drachm. I can't even imagine how light that must be – much lighter than a grain of sand.

Sister Agnes makes us repeat over and over again, all the lengths from inches to miles, all the nautical distances from fathoms to leagues, all the areas from perches to acres, all the fluids up to gallons and all the weights up to tons, until we can recite them perfectly. She says we need to learn the practical measures that we use on the farm before we can move on to other Arithmetic.

She gets pretty worked up during our weights' and measures' drills, walking in between the rows of desks, hitting them one by one with her cane. 'Getting into a rhythm helps your memory,' she says. It really helps mine. I haven't had the cane once from Sister Agnes, except when she walks past hitting my desk.

I can't say the same for Sister Ambrose and Sister Cornelius. I don't think either of them likes teaching indoors, where they both turn into monsters and so do we.

Sister Ambrose teaches History and Geography, usually at the same time. She has a small collection of maps and charts that she pulls down in front of the blackboard. We slip easily from learning about the rivers of Africa to the kings and queens of England. It all depends on the order of the charts and maps. It can get a bit confusing at times.

Sister Ambrose also lisps but doesn't seem to know that she does. When we repeat the names of the Stuart kings with a lisp, she hits the chart over and over again with her cane. 'No, no, no!' she says. 'Why can't you say "James" and "Charles" properly? Hold out your hands!' She then walks between each row, giving us all two cuts of the cane on each hand. We're not really making fun of her, just repeating what she says.

She also takes us for Sport: athletics and rugby in winter, and in the warmer months, cricket and swimming (if there's enough water in the creek). 'If I didn't become a nun, I would've been a champion swimmer,' she told us one morning at milking duty. I'd thought her broad shoulders and strong arms must've been from milking cows. She's also the farmer among the nuns and happily oversees all the milking and farm duties.

Sister Cornelius teaches us English and Science, and is so small that she needs a stepladder to write at the top of the blackboard. She also supervises all the work in the veggie garden and orchard, and knows the Latin names of everything that grows there.

In the classroom, she keeps her cane on the desk, ready for action. She calmly starts each English lesson by reading a poem. Some poems are so long, like *The Rime of the Ancient Mariner*, that we start playing up or nodding off. That's when she gets mad, grabbing the cane and hitting anyone who's not paying attention. She looks really funny when she gets mad – more like an angry leprechaun than a nun. That's when we start laughing and she starts shouting and throwing things – books, chalk, dusters, boxes – anything she can lay her hands on. Whatever starts out at the front of the classroom, ends up down the back after English. It takes ages to clean up after Sister Cornelius.

Fortunately, she teaches Science outside – in the orchard, in the paddocks, the veggie garden, down by the creek and, when it's raining, in the barn. She loves doing experiments and observing or dissecting anything that moves and lots that don't. She's obsessed with the weather, so every day we take it in turns to record rainfall, temperature, humidity, air pressure, wind speed and direction, using a variety of instruments that she bought, made or borrowed from Henry, the caretaker.

Although Sunday Mass isn't technically a lesson, Sister Agnes turns it into one. She picks out different Latin phrases from the mass every week for us to learn, as well as a new hymn to sing. She writes the numbers of the hymns on the blackboard so that we can find the right ones in our hymn books and practise beforehand if we have time. The hymns must've all been written using the same music because they all sound the same.

Father Brian arrives early on Sundays to hear our confessions, one by one, as we line up on the verandah ready for Mass. There's no privacy but we're used to that. To keep it short, we're only allowed to confess one sin each per week. Not a bad system. It's easy enough to come up with one sin to confess, I have so many to choose from. And penance is only ever a few Our Fathers and Hail Marys. Hardly a challenge.

Father Brian speaks Latin so fast that Mass is over in half an hour. He breezes through the epistle, gospel and sermon, and before we know it, he's popping the body of Christ into our mouths at Communion. After he gives his final blessing, he bows to the Three Sisters, puts on his hat, and then climbs up into his sulky for the trip back to town.

Sister Agnes is always smiling as she waves goodbye to Father Brian. I'm not sure if that's because she likes him or she's glad to see the back of him. She seems to be just as happy after he's gone.

KIT'S LETTER

I started to lose track of the days, and hadn't had many classroom lessons because it had been a cold, dry winter. You don't need to be Thomas Edison to see there was too much work to be done on the farm to be reading poetry, reciting the kings and queens of England, doing sums and writing stories. As Sister Agnes explained: 'It's all a matter of priorities – we need to eat, drink, wash and keep warm, and we can't do that if we don't milk cows, cart water, slaughter sheep and chickens, grow our own fruit and vegetables, collect eggs, chop and split wood, and make charcoal. It's ten miles to the nearest village, and even if we had the money, we'd have to drive to a much bigger town to buy enough food to feed all of us.' So, we have to work outside much more than inside doing schoolwork. But I wasn't complaining; I was enjoying the hard, physical work of the Farm.

It was Pete's thirteenth birthday, and Mrs Lucas baked him a chocolate cake (as she does on everyone's birthday), with thirteen very short and well-used candles. Pete also got to go into town with Henry. If your birthday happens to fall on a day when Henry is picking up the mail and basic supplies, you get to go with him in either the truck (if there's enough charcoal to run it), or the horse-drawn cart. He only drives into town once a fortnight so you have to be lucky for that to be on the same day as your birthday. Presents aren't allowed at the Farm, not even for birthdays. Any parcels sent to us are marked 'return to sender' and posted back to where they came from.

We're only allowed to receive one letter each

month. I could write a letter as well if I had the time or if I managed to teach myself how to write in the dark. It's lamps out at eight o'clock. Saves on postage stamps, I suppose.

My first letter from Kit arrived; postmarked 'Glebe, 6 August 1931' it had taken three weeks to get here. I waited until I was alone in one of the paddocks, collecting cow dung, before I stopped to read it:

Dear Joe,

I hope you get this letter in time for your birthday. Mum's still going to make you a cake but because she's not allowed to send it to you, we're all going to eat it and Mum said I can blow out the candles.

I won a scholarship but not to St Bart's, I made sure I failed that exam. I'm going to Sydney Boys High School next year. No boarding school for me. At least Mum and Dad won't have to worry about me running away like you did. I'm saving up to buy a bicycle so I can ride to school every day. I can wear trousers if I like. I hate wearing shorts – everyone laughs at my hairy legs. Were your legs as hairy as mine when you were eleven?

Noni and Fred are getting engaged in two years when Noni turns eighteen. Dad won't let her get married until she's twenty-one, but I overheard them say something about eloping. Looks like I'm the only one not planning to run away.

I'm still doing your paper run. I don't think Mr Thompson is paying me enough and that's what Dad says too. Do you want to take over again when you get back? Mum and Dad don't fight as much as before, hardly ever. They've been raking in the money. The punters are on a losing streak. All the long-shots have been getting up.

I can't wait to see you again – just four months to go. It'll be Christmas before you know it. We can put up the tree together just like old times. Uncle George said he'll drop one off the week before Christmas like he always does.

Harry's given up the egg business, he says it's too much trouble. He hates getting the train out to Rooty Hill all by himself. He's been mugged twice and had all his eggs stolen.

Don't forget about rumble time because I won't.

Your loving brother,
Kit

PS Do nuns really shave their heads?

PPS Dad went to the doctor again today. There's something wrong with him but he won't talk about it and Mum won't tell me anything.

Kit's letter made me feel homesick, damn it! I folded up the letter and put it in my pocket, then shovelled more cow dung into the wheelbarrow for the veggie garden. I kept an eye out for mushrooms but because it hadn't rained for a while, there weren't any. Just lots of cow dung.

FEAST DAY

It was a special feast day of the Blessed Virgin Mary, and Sister Agnes told us that if God hadn't answered our prayers, we could pray to Mary for help because she was his mother. Being Catholic, I understand that God has extraordinary powers – he made the world, didn't he? But how can your mother be a virgin unless you're adopted? Harry and I talked about some of these things last year, and he'd assured me that Mary might've been a virgin before she fell pregnant with Jesus, but even if it was an immaculate conception, nobody who has given birth could still be a virgin. I see his point but I have a few unanswered questions, not all to do with religion, and I'm not sure who to ask.

To celebrate the Virgin Mary's feast day, Mrs Lucas was cooking up a feast for dinner. All going to plan, yabby, rabbit and chook would be on the menu, but we had to catch and kill them first.

'When the hens stop layin' they're only good for one thing,' Mrs Lucas said.

I watched in horror as Lance wrung the neck of the first chook then dropped it on the ground to pick up the next one. He wrung its neck with a quick twist of his large man hands.

'Here, Joe, I kept these last two for ya. Ya not scared of a couple o' chooks, are ya?'

'No!'

'Joe's scared o' the chickens! *Bok bok bok bok bok bok*!' Lance strutted around, flapping his elbows and making chook noises.

When I was little, I watched Dad wring a chook's neck in our backyard. It was the last one we had left – all the others had died. Her name was Cleopatra.

'I've got to help Henry skin some rabbits. I'm late – he'll be waiting for me,' I said, running off with Pete and Charlie following close behind.

'Why didn't ya do it?' Charlie asked.

'He didn't hafta if he didn't want. Lance was bein' an idiot,' said Pete, who always sticks up for me, no matter what.

'Ya still shoulda done it,' said Charlie.

'Well, I'm sick of doing everything that Lance tells me to!'

Henry was kneeling down on a patch of grass outside the barn, skinning a dead rabbit. While we'd been busy milking cows early that morning, Henry had been out shooting rabbits. 'Easy targets,' he said. 'There they were in the veggie garden, munchin' away on the spinach. Four shots is all it took; scared the others off – they disappeared quick smart. As soon as they came back, I was waitin' for 'em an' banged a couple more.' Henry cut chunks of flesh off the skinned rabbit and handed them to me. 'They're for the yabby traps. Go down to the creek an' see what ya can catch for the feast tonight. Yabbies love fresh meat – works every time. I'll skin these other bunnies and get 'em to Mrs Lucas for the stew.'

Charlie and Pete got the yabby traps out of the barn while I carried the fresh chunks of rabbit meat. They felt warm and slimy, and I tried not to look at them. As we walked down the track to the creek, I thought about Kit's letter. I could feel it in my side pocket and it was reassuring to hear the sound of the paper scrunching as I walked.

We sat on the creek bank, threading chunks of meat onto hooks inside the yabby traps. After doing up the catches, we lifted the traps by their ropes, swung them backwards and forwards and threw them into the water. Sitting back down on the grassy bank, we watched the traps sink slowly.

'It's my birthday on Thursday,' I said.

'Mrs Lucas is gunna be busy bakin' another cake!' said Pete.

'How old will ya be?' Charlie asked.

'Thirteen.' I threw a rock into the creek but instead of skimming the surface, it sank.

'Idiot, ya'll scare all the yabbies away!' Lance said as he sat down on the grass next to me. There were some ducks swimming further up the creek, taking it in turns to flap their wings and splash water. Lance threw rocks at them and they flew off. I went to say something to him but changed my mind.

'Anyone ever tell ya 'bout Racin' the Moon?' he asked.

'What's that?' I said, trying not to sound too interested.

'It's a Farm tradition, got banned by Sister Agnes 'bout two years ago. Every spring, at the start o' the first full moon, Henry'd take some boys on a night hike to say prayers on top o' the mountain. That's what he told Sister Agnes an' she believed 'im.'

'As if she'd believe they'd climb up there to pray!' Pete said, laughing.

He had a point.

'Probably hoped you'd run away and never come back,' I said.

We all laughed. Lance gave me a filthy look.

'When ya go Racin' the Moon, ya hafta leave as

soon as ya can after the moon comes up, then try an' beat it to the top o' the mountain. I went with Henry an' the boys two years ago. Henry an' I used hatchets to cut all the vines an' branches that had grown over the track from the year before. It's rockier an' steeper than ya think. We got down on our hands an' knees in some places. Henry showed us a secret cave with rock paintin' done by some Aboriginals who used to come up every year from the coast. Took us three hours to get to the top but it was worth it.'

'Did you beat the moon?' I asked.

'We sure did!'

'What did ya do when ya got there?' Charlie asked.

'Probably howled at the moon,' I said, laughing.

Lance hit me across the head. 'I've just 'bout had enough o' ya. We didn't howl at the moon — we told stories 'bout murders, ghosts, yowies an' stupid boys like you. Billy was one o' the new boys. He got spooked an' tried to run back down the mountain, but he ran the wrong way. Before I could stop 'im, he ran right off the top o' the cliff. Tried to find 'im on our way back an' for the next couple o' days, but couldn't. Henry an' the police from Wollongong came with some dogs – still no luck. 'Bout a year later, an Aboriginal tracker was helpin' police look for two escapees from the prison farm near Mount Kembla when they came across some bones.'

I was hanging off every word as Lance told the story of Racing the Moon; not that I believed everything he said. I was excited by the danger of it and could picture myself up there on the mountain. I wanted to climb that mountain and see the full moon up close.

Back home, I used to climb the old oak tree with Kit to hide from Dad and watch the moon rise above the rooftops. Some nights, I'd lie awake in bed for hours watching the moon through my window. Every part of my body wanted to race that moon.

As Lance stood up, he tripped over me trying to pull up one of the yabby traps. When he lifted it out of the water, it was empty. 'Best leave 'em for another hour or so. The chooks are ready for pluckin'. Let's go!' he said, waiting for Charlie, Pete and me to go past, which wasn't like him at all. Lance always likes to be first, leading, telling everybody else what to do.

When we got back to the house, there were four

headless chooks hanging upside down on the clothes line with small pools of blood below on the grass. Lance came out of the kitchen carrying a bucket of water and set it down near them. 'Put 'em in the hot water first to loosen up the feathers then they'll come out easy,' he said. 'Back in a minute – I hafta take a piss.'

I'd rather get one of my teeth pulled out than to pluck a dead chook. I watched Charlie and Pete put their chooks under the hot water, and then it was my turn. I put Cleopatra to the back of my mind as best I could, and pushed my chook under for a half a minute or so, then lifted it out and started plucking. I could hear Lance's voice nearby and some boys laughing. When I turned around, I saw Lance holding a letter. I stopped plucking to listen.

'I hate wearin' shorts – everyone laughs at me hairy legs. Were yer legs as hairy as mine when ya were eleven? Noni an' Fred are getting engaged in two years when Noni turns eighteen. Woo, woo! I'd like to get a bit o' that tart,' he said.

My mind just snapped. I ran at Lance like a charging bull, ramming him right in the guts. 'You bastard!' I said, grabbing my letter. 'And you're a thief!'

No sooner had I put the letter in my pocket than Lance king hit me – knocking me out cold.

I woke up on the sick bed inside the house with Sister Cornelius waving something putrid under my nose.

'You've got a lump the size of Queensland above that eye,' she said. I tried to get up but the room started spinning and there was more than one Sister Cornelius. 'You know fighting is forbidden.'

'He started it.'

'It doesn't matter who started it, fighting is a sin,' she said, bathing the lump on my head.

'Ow, that hurts!'

'Your eye's swelling up – it'll be black and blue by morning. Sister Agnes said you'll have to go into another work team until things settle down between you and Lance. I'll be back in a minute. Don't move.' She picked up the dish of water and left.

I looked up at the crucifix on the white wall above my head but it hurt too much. Closing my eyes, I tried to go to sleep. I might've scored a black eye and a massive headache, but at least I had Kit's letter safely in my pocket.

MY BIRTHDAY

I hated being in another work team but I didn't miss Lance. That bastard got off lightly for knocking me out – all he had to do was say a few lousy rosaries. He told Sister Agnes that I started it. I didn't bother trying to explain to her about Kit's letter and how Lance made fun of it in front of the other boys. I just wanted to forget about it. I missed working with my mates, especially Pete. I'd been dizzy, sore and out of sorts for a few days. Sister Cornelius said I had a concussion.

I also missed the special feast day dinner. Pete told me how Mrs Lucas boiled up the yabbies in a big pot over the kitchen fire. I was sound asleep in sick bay and he wasn't allowed to wake me up. He said the yabbies tasted like a cross between fish and chicken, only better. If they were better than the chicken soup that I'd had, they must've been pretty good.

We had rabbit stew for dinner the night I got out of sick bay. Henry shot and skinned eight more rabbits that he'd spotted around the veggie garden so there was plenty to go around. When I took the first pile of washed dishes into the kitchen to be wiped and put away, Mrs Lucas was icing a cake. 'Off ya go!' she said, trying to hide the cake. As I walked backwards out of the kitchen, my mouth was watering. Chocolate cake is my favourite and I couldn't wait to try it.

As I sat on the bench in between Charlie and Pete, Sister Agnes announced that it was my birthday – 3 September, the third day of spring. When Mrs Lucas walked onto the verandah with the cake and thirteen brand-new flickering candles, everyone started singing 'Happy Birthday' to me. Everyone, that is, except Lance.

After I blew out the candles, Mrs Lucas handed me a knife. Before the knife had even touched the plate, she grabbed it from me. I don't know what she thought I was going to do with it. It's not like I wanted to stab anyone, except maybe Lance – nothing fatal, just a flesh wound. But all I really wanted was some cake. I waited impatiently for the biggest slice, which always goes to the birthday boy. It was the second-best chocolate cake I'd ever tasted. Mum's is still the best.

Lying in bed that night after lamps out, I couldn't sleep. I kept thinking about Racing the Moon – how I'd go about it, what I'd take, who I'd ask to come with me. I didn't believe all of Lance's story, especially the bit about the boy falling off the cliff and dying. I think he made that up just to scare us and put us off going. I've always loved a challenge – the riskier the better.

But to race the moon to the top of the mountain and look at it close up – that would be magic!

I decided that in the morning, I'd ask Sister Cornelius when the next full moon would be. She knows all about that kind of thing.

GETTING READY
CHAPTER 30

'Should be a full moon tonight,' Sister Cornelius replied, gazing up at the sky like she was looking for some kind of sign.

'Thanks, Sister,' I said. Sooner than I'd expected, but when you get an opportunity, you just have to grab it. I had to tell Pete and Charlie – there was no time to lose.

They were in the kitchen finishing wiping up duty. Mrs Lucas was standing at the stove with her back to us, stirring a big pot. I grabbed a tea towel and started helping so as not to look suspicious. 'This is it – the first full moon in spring,' I whispered. 'Are you going to come Racing the Moon with me tonight?'

'Count me in,' said Pete.

'Me too,' said Charlie. Anyone else comin'?'

'Just the three of us – it's better that way,' I said. 'And don't tell anyone, especially Lance. If we want to do it properly, we'll have to be ready to leave straight after lamps out. We'll need paper and matches in case we want to light a fire.'

'An' some extra paper to stuff down our clothes to keep warm, said Pete. 'I've done it lots o' times – works really well.'

'Won't we make too much noise with paper stuffed down our clothes?' Charlie asked.

'I'm talkin' 'bout up on the mountain. It gets cold up there ya know,' Pete replied.

'What if we get caught before we even get to the mountain?' Charlie asked, sounding worried.

'We'll get the cane, say some rosaries, do a few extra chores, and then we'll go Racing the Moon next month,' I replied. 'Don't worry Charlie, if all goes to plan we'll be back before the sun comes up. No-one will even know we were gone. If Lance could do it, we can too.' I was getting excited just talking about it.

'Stop talkin' an' wipe up!' Mrs Lucas called out, watching us like a hawk as she stirred the pot.

I could see a box of matches on the floor next to the fireplace. 'Something smells good!' I said, wandering over to Mrs Lucas and giving her a cheesy smile before looking in the pot.

'I'm boilin' up some chicken carcasses to make soup for dinner tonight.'

'Yum!' I replied, looking at the bony remains of half a dozen chooks boiling away inside the big pot, trying not to think about poor Cleopatra. 'I can't wait to try it,' I lied, casually kicking the box of matches towards Pete. He dropped his tea towel on top of the matches then picked them both up at the same time, putting the matches in his pocket. We wiped up the last of the cutlery and then hung the wet tea towels out on the clothes-line to dry.

There were only two newspapers left in Henry's

shed, so Pete and I snuck into the classroom and, while Charlie stood guard, we ripped out as many blank pages from the back of exercise books as we could in less than a minute. The rest of the boys were setting off to do their morning chores. We ran to our cabin and threw the paper under our beds, and then took a short cut through the orchard, arriving just in time to grab some hoes and start digging in the veggie garden before Sister Cornelius noticed we were late. Four teams were working there that morning – the other four teams were in the paddocks with Henry and Sister Ambrose for stock duty.

After tilling the soil and making furrows, we planted rows and rows of seeds: beans, carrots, beetroot, parsnip, turnips, peas, spinach and pumpkin. We also had to fix the wire around the veggie garden to keep the rabbits out, before we could head off for lunch under the flame trees.

We had our usual lunch of bread, butter and jam, as well as oranges, freshly picked from the orchard. After saying prayers and singing hymns, the four teams who had been working in the veggie garden swapped with those on stock duty, so we made our way to the paddocks with Sister Ambrose.

Henry was already in the sheep paddock, waiting for us. He's a real farmer who knows everything there is to know about running a farm. 'We need to crutch the sheep to keep 'em dry, less likely to get fly strike. When we've finished crutchin', we hafta trim their hooves. What we don't get done this afternoon, we'll finish off tomorra.'

The morning group had crutched and trimmed the hooves of half the flock and we had to do the other half, so we herded the thirty two sheep into a pen. Henry grabbed a sheep, holding it firmly between his legs.

'Ya hafta hold 'em firmly but not too tight. It might take two o' ya to hold 'em down until ya get used to it. I'm not shearin' all the wool off − just crutchin' 'er. Watch how I clip the wool from 'round the backside … top o' the legs … an' all 'round the tail. Done! Now for the hooves.' Henry put the shears down and picked up some clippers. 'First, dig out any dirt between the toes then trim the nail 'round the toe an' heel, but not too much that ya make 'em bleed. Trim the nail nice an' flat, but if ya need to smooth it off, ya can use a file.' Henry finished trimming the other hooves and then pushed the sheep on her way.

Each team had eight sheep, so we took it in turns to crutch our sheep and trim their hooves while Henry and Sister Ambrose watched and gave advice. Two of my teammates had to hold my sheep still, which was no easy task, while I started crutching her. I sheared slowly, being careful not to clip anything that I shouldn't. Trimming her hooves was just as hard, and I was scared that I was going to trim too much off and make her bleed. My team ran out of time and didn't get to trim all of our sheep's hooves. That privilege had to wait another day.

We were five minutes late for milking duty. As I sat on the stool and squeezed my cow's teats, all I could think about was running up that mountain and getting close enough to touch that moon. It was lucky it wasn't shower day because we wouldn't have had time – it was already starting to get dark.

The chicken soup that Mrs Lucas made for dinner had more veggies in it than chicken but tasted great.

There were six loaves of freshly baked bread, which didn't take thirty-two boys very long to demolish. I managed to sneak a slice into my pocket when no-one was watching. Charlie and Pete did the same. There were no Bible stories and hymns around the campfire that night – it was too late. By the time we'd finished washing and wiping up, it was time for bed.

RACING THE MOON

CHAPTER 31

We wore our overalls and jumpers to bed, ready to go. It seemed to take ages for Sister Cornelius to turn off the kerosene lamps and then call out her usual: 'Good night and God bless.' As soon as I thought she'd gone, I counted to a hundred then jumped out of bed.

'What are you doing?' she called out. She must have been standing there, watching.

'I just need to use the bucket, Sister.'

'Hurry up.' She stood in the doorway waiting for me. 'Why are you wearing your overalls?' she asked as I walked past on my way back to bed.

'I'm cold, Sister.'

'Take them off before you go to bed.'

I undid my overalls and pretended to take them off before getting into bed. It was dark enough inside the cabin for her not to see exactly what I was doing. *This is going to take longer than I thought.*

In bed again, I waited impatiently for as long as I could. Sliding onto the floor, I grabbed my case from under the bed and put it on top, pulling my sheet and blanket up over it. *Perfect.* Then I quietly slid the two newspapers out from under my bed.

Charlie was in the bed next to me. When I squeezed his hand, he slid onto the floor, put his case on the bed and pulled up the covers, just like I'd done. I didn't need to get Pete – he was already out of bed, waiting for us, clutching the pages we'd torn out of the exercise books.

'Who's there?' Lance called out from his bed at the back of the cabin.

I gave Charlie a nudge. 'It's me, Charlie. I hafta take a piss.'

'Is anyone with ya?'

'Just me,' Pete said. I'm bustin' to go too – must've been that chicken soup.'

'Well, hurry up, I wanna go too,' Lance replied.

There was only one door in and out of the cabin. I went first, crawling onto the verandah then running to the barn where I waited for Pete and Charlie. I crouched down, looking all around – the coast was clear. I was surprised at how light it was. Looking up, I saw that the full moon was already higher than me – we didn't have another minute to lose. Pete ran across to the barn first, then Charlie.

'Let's go before Lance realises we've gone,' I whispered. I ran as fast as I could down the dirt track, over the second cattle stop, past the orchard and veggie garden then down the narrow track to the creek.

'Damn it, I forgot about the creek!' I said, waiting for Charlie and Pete to catch up. 'There's no way around – we'll have to cross it.' I folded one of the newspapers and put it under my jumper so it wouldn't get wet. I gave Charlie the other newspaper while Pete shoved the wad of torn pages under his overalls and jumper.

'I know where there's a tree fallen across the creek a bit further downstream. I'll show ya,' said Charlie. Pete and I followed him along the creek bank to the fallen tree. We rolled up our overalls and walked along the partly submerged log, but it didn't go all the way across, so we jumped into the water and waded the rest of the way.

We ran back upstream along the creek bank to the start of the mountain track. There was no sign of Lance anywhere. My feet were cold but I was used to going barefoot. I'd toughened up during my last three months at the Farm. 'There's my marker – this is the track,' I said, pointing to a page from my Geography exercise book that I'd stuck on a bush like a flag. *There's no turning back*, I thought.

Leading the way through the bush, I was surprised at how noisy it was. Crickets were chirping all around, but not as loudly as the kookaburras that I hoped weren't laughing at us. I could also hear animals and lizards scurrying away into the bush. It was light enough to see the golden wattle still in flower as well as gum trees and banksias, tangled in a maze of dead lantana and blackberries, which were harder to spot but kept catching on my overalls and jumper. I could hear Charlie's and Pete's cries behind me as they got snagged on the lantana and blackberries as well.

Every noise we made seemed louder up there on the mountain. The bush was getting thicker and I could only just see the track. The moon was still higher than us but we were starting to close the gap. There were strange animal noises coming from higher up in the trees. 'Sounds like a couple of possums having a fight,' I called out to Pete and Charlie.

'I reckon they could be matin',' Pete said, and we all laughed.

Not looking where I was going, I tripped and fell, landing hard on some sharp rocks.

'You alright, mate?' he asked.

'Just a graze,' I said, rubbing my bleeding hands on my overalls. I'd also kicked the big toe on my right foot and half the toenail was hanging off. It hurt like hell but I didn't let on. Nothing was going to stop me from Racing the Moon.

It was getting rockier and steeper, and I had to concentrate really hard to stay on the track, which began to zigzag up the mountainside. Suddenly, there was a rock face in front of me and no way around it. Looking up, I had to feel my way using my hands and feet, finding places in the rock to hold onto and pull myself up. My hands were stinging and my toe was killing me, but I kept going. Grabbing onto the top of the ledge, I slipped and almost fell, breaking off bits of rock that hit Charlie on the head.

'Ow!' he cried. 'I don't think I can do this!'

'Yes, you can. You're almost at the ledge,' I called out, pulling myself up onto the rock. I held out my hand for Charlie to grab onto. He groaned as I pulled and Pete pushed him up onto the ledge. Pete didn't need any help – he climbed up the rock as if he'd done it a thousand times before.

I climbed up onto a boulder and looked around. The full moon was almost level with my eyes. 'There's the moon – let's go!'

I ran up the winding track through low-lying scrub and into a forest of gum trees but, thankfully, no more lantana or blackberries.

Can't be too much further, I thought. *Feels like we've been climbing for hours.* It had been a long day and I was getting tired and starting to slow down. It was really hard trying to climb a mountain at night with only the moonlight to help find your way. 'How's it going back there?'

'I'm lovin' this!' Pete said.

'I didn't like that cliff. I thought I was gunna fall off and break me neck,' Charlie said, huffing and puffing. He's a big boy, almost as big as Pete and me put together, and he gets out of breath easily.

Up ahead, through the trees, was a bright circle of light. As I ran towards the moon, I could see that it was still higher than we were, damn it! 'It's going to beat us!' I shouted. Then I heard a loud, cracking sound above me. As I looked up a large branch was breaking off a gum tree. I dived out of the way just in time. It missed me and fell across the track. Pete climbed over it and Charlie followed him.

'That branch just missed ya by a few inches,' Pete said.

'That's what Henry calls a widow-maker,' said Charlie.

'Must be my lucky day,' I said, taking off again and following the track along the edge of the cliff. Part of the rock face up ahead was darker than the rest. As I got closer, I saw that it was the opening to a cave. 'This must be the cave that Lance was talking about – the one with the Aboriginal rock paintings. We can take a look on the way back.'

After climbing up some rocks and another steep section of the track, I looked across and saw that I was finally level with the moon. It spurred me on and I started to run. It didn't take long until I was up higher than it was.

Nothing can stop me now, I thought. Drunk with excitement, I ran up a rocky slope, jumping from one rock to the next, some slippery with moss. It then got so steep that I had to climb on all fours. Scrambling up onto a clearing, I could finally see the end in sight. I ran over rocks and low-lying scrub, racing the moon to the top of the mountain, drawn by that magical ball of light. 'I did it!' I shouted. Pete arrived next then Charlie came a few minutes later.

'We beat the moon, we did it!' Jumping up and down with joy, we cheered and whistled, hugging each other.

The moon was shining right in front of us – I felt like I could almost reach out and touch it. I could even see its craters – they didn't look like a man's face at all. Looking down, I saw that a light was on in the main house of the Farm but could only just make out the caretaker's cottage where Henry and Mrs Lucas lived on the far side of the barn.

'The nuns are up late,' I said.

'Do ya think they've found out we're gone?' Pete asked.

I looked around, checking for any other lights and movement. 'I don't think so. They're probably still up saying their prayers,' I said, confidently.

We sat on top of the mountain, eating bread and telling ghost stories. When we couldn't think of any more scary stories, we started telling jokes instead.

I went first: 'What's brown and white, brown and white, brown and white, brown and white?'

'A cow?' said Charlie.

'No – a nun rolling down the hill. Ha, ha, ha!' How we laughed at our stupid jokes, and didn't notice the moon disappearing behind the clouds that had been building up, until the sky was dark – too dark to see – too dark to make our way back. We collected sticks and branches, breaking them up to make a fire, then scrunched up some of the newspaper from under our jumpers, putting it in the pile of sticks. I lit the paper with the matches I'd stolen from the kitchen. As soon as the fire was burning hot, we threw on a couple of bigger branches to keep it going.

'It's too dangerous to go down the mountain in the dark,' I said, happy to have an excuse to stay there all night. 'But we'll have to wake up early and get back in time for milking duty. We'll keep warmer if we stay close to the fire and closer together.' Then we sat around the fire, reliving every moment of our amazing journey.

The last thing I remember before falling asleep

was watching the glowing embers of the dying fire as I snuggled into Charlie's back, and Pete snuggled into mine to keep warm.

WAKING UP
CHAPTER 32

In the damp, dim light of early morning I began
to stir. Judging by Henry's rooster that I could
hear crowing back at the Farm, it was only about five
o'clock. Charlie was out like a light – it takes more
than a rooster to wake him up. But I couldn't see Pete
anywhere.

'Pete?' There was no answer. I stood up, looking
all around. 'Cooee!' I called out, my voice echoing
through the mountain air, setting off the kookaburras

on their early morning laughing session. I waited for Pete's reply but there was none, so I tried again. Still nothing.

'What's up?' Charlie asked, sleepily.

'I can't find Pete,' I replied, looking around for some sign of him, something to indicate he'd been there, but I couldn't find anything.

Charlie and I searched the mountain top together, but there was no sign of Pete. Two gunshots rang out, echoing all around. *Probably Henry shooting rabbits in the veggie garden,* I thought.

I went to the edge of the cliff and looked down. It was the opposite side of the mountain to the Farm. Water was flowing over a rock ledge, through the mist and into the creek below – it was the waterfall that Pete and I had swum under. On the far side of the creek, there was something lying on the grass, but I couldn't make out what it was. *Probably a log that washed up,* I thought.

Charlie and I headed back down the mountain track, looking for Pete at every turn. The rocks were slippery and, at times, I could only see a couple of yards in front because the mist was so thick. Following the track along the edge of the cliff, I kept looking down and almost lost my balance a couple of times. When the track stopped suddenly, I had to slide down onto the ledge below. As I waited for Charlie to catch up, I was getting impatient and more and more worried about Pete.

I went down another steep section, sliding on my bum most of the way, then followed the narrow track to the cave that we'd found on the way up. 'Cooee!' I called. There was a long echo but no reply. I went in a bit further, but it was too dark to see anything. When I came back out, I met up with Charlie who was looking over the ledge.

'What's that?' he said, pointing at what looked like somebody lying on the grass next to the creek.

I took off again, following the track around the cliff and down through the forest of gum trees, jumping over the large branch that had fallen and just missed me the night before. I scrambled down the mountain as fast as I could, not always keeping to the winding track. I slid down the big rock face that we'd climbed up before, landing hard and very close to the edge of the cliff. My body was aching but I kept going. I left the track, pushing my way past lantana and blackberry bushes, jumping and sliding over rocks, taking the shortest possible route down to the creek. I splashed my way through the icy-cold water and then stopped.

In the early morning light, I could see the mop of brown hair that I knew so well. It was Pete. I think I'd known it up on the mountain – I just didn't want to believe it. I knelt down and touched his cold, damp hair.

'G'day mate, where have ya been?'

I fell back in fright as if I'd been pushed. 'Jesus, you scared the living daylights out of me! You're alive, you bastard!'

'Sure am,' Pete said, sitting up, stretching and yawning.

'What are you doing all the way down here?' I asked.

'I needed t'ave a piss, but it was too dark to see where I was goin'. Got worried I might fall off the cliff like Billy did, so I crawled around on me hands an' knees until I found a safe spot. There I was havin' a piss, when I heard this terrible screechin' – sounded like animals tryin' to kill each other. When I saw the yellow eyes – real evil they were, just like me stepdad's – I bolted. I fell over a few times, but apart from that, I didn't stop until I reached the creek.'

'You're a lucky bugger, you know that?' I said, putting my arm around him. I looked up at the mountain, watching as it broke through the mist. 'I can't believe we climbed all the way to the top. Look at the size of it!'

'I thought ya were dead!' Charlie called out, running towards us. There was a bright-yellow crescent of light rising up through the trees behind him.

'The sun's coming up!' I shouted.

We ran back up the dirt track, past the charcoal pits, orchard and veggie garden, took a short cut through the flame trees to miss the cattle stop, and then crossed the track, running into the barn as fast as we could, even though we knew we were already late for milking duty.

MORE LIES
CHAPTER 33

'Where have you boys been? These poor cows are about to burst. If they get infected, it'll be your fault!' Sister Ambrose looked like she was about to burst too.

'Sorry, Sister.' I stared at my wet overalls and muddy feet, and saw that my big toe was bleeding again.

'Don't "sorry" me! It's the cows you should be apologising to. Where have you been?' She looked the three of us up and down.

'We had an accident emptying the night buckets, Sister. It went all over us – it was disgusting,' I said, recalling the first time I was on bucket duty. 'We had to go down to the creek to wash it off. That's why our overalls are wet.' Charlie and Pete nodded in support. I could tell they were impressed with my lie.

'Did you spill both buckets? That's quite a coincidence or else very clumsy of you, don't you think?'

'They were full to the brim, Sister,' I replied. 'One was already overflowing.'

'Alright then, go wash your hands and then give these cows' teats a wipe ready for milking. Don't forget the leg ropes or they'll kick the buckets over. You won't have time for breakfast this morning.' Sister Ambrose patted my cow on the rump and walked out of the barn.

As I washed my hands, Lance walked past, swinging an empty milk bucket. 'Liars! None o' ya were on bucket duty this mornin'. Charlie an' Pete were s'posed to be helpin' me but didn't show. I know where ya all were. I got caught last night chasin' after ya! When Sister Cornelius followed me back to the cabin, she had a quick look 'round at all the beds – everyone seemed to be there. Nice work, puttin' ya cases under ya covers. Ya owe me!' he said, storming off.

I sat down on the stool with my head against the cow's belly, my hands on her two back teats, and started milking like there was no tomorrow. She must've been sore with that swollen udder because she kept turning her head and mooing at me. I half-filled the bucket in no time and then started on the front teats. It didn't take long before I was carrying a bucket of milk to the kitchen. It was too late to do any separating.

I missed out on porridge for breakfast but managed to grab a slice of bread and a cup of strong tea. I stood on the verandah, sipping my tea and looking up at the mountain. *What a night!* I thought. *I'm thirteen years old – I've had a successful egg business and paper run, I've won the Glebe Billycart Derby, blue ribbons for athletics, a cricket trophy – and I've just finished Racing the Moon. To top it off, I didn't get caught. The world is still my oyster!*

After breakfast, I headed to the sheep paddock with the rest of my team to finish off trimming the hooves on our sheep. As soon as we'd finished, Henry asked us to check for any maggots or lice in the wool because he'd found some lice on the two rams that he'd crutched that morning.

It was easy work, just a matter of parting the wool and checking for any tiny creatures clinging to the fibres. The sheep seemed to like all the attention and didn't even try to get away.

'As soon as yer finished, ya can move the sheep into the new paddock – there's more feed for 'em there,' Henry called out.

Although I heard everything that Henry said, my mind was elsewhere. 'Do you miss Racing the Moon?' I asked him.

'What are ya talkin' about?'

'Racing the Moon – you know – used to be a Farm tradition until Sister Agnes put a stop to it two years ago.'

'I don't know nothin' 'bout no "Racin' the Moon", but there was a young boy named Billy who died here two years ago. Lance had just arrived at the Farm – trouble from the start he was, but the nuns couldn't see it. He an' some other boys snuck out one night an' climbed the mountain. Lance told us afterwards that Billy lost his footin' an' fell off the cliff. Terrible tragedy. The police were called an' eventually found his body. Sister Agnes an' Father Brian believed Lance's story. I've got me doubts. I'll be glad to see the back of 'im in a few days. He's turnin' fourteen, ya know. Can't stay at the Farm when yer an adult.'

Lance had lied to us about Racing the Moon and we'd believed him. Henry had nothing to do with it. We could've died up there on the mountain – but we didn't. We all made it to the top and back again safely. It was the hardest thing I'd ever done in my life. I still believed in Racing the Moon, even if it was kind of a lie to begin with.

As we let the sheep out of the holding pen to take them to the new paddock, Henry called out: 'Can ya grab a couple o' bags o' charcoal from the barn to put in the truck on ya way back? I hafta pick up a bull from a farmer down the road to breed with some of our cows to keep their milk supply goin'.'

By the time we'd finished pouring the bags of charcoal into the gas converter fitted to the side of the truck's engine, it was too late for Henry to pick up the bull. It was also looking like rain. While we were having dinner, it started to pour.

It rained for six days straight. We had lesson after lesson with the Three Sisters. I'd never been in the classroom for so long before. Sister Cornelius finally finished reading *The Rime of the Ancient Mariner*, and then we wrote stories and letters. Half the class needed new exercise books – there were no blank pages left in their old ones – they'd all been ripped out.

'Well done!' Sister Cornelius said as she handed out new books. 'Keep up the good work!'

I wrote a story in my new English exercise book about Racing the Moon. I changed the names of the boys so Sister Cornelius wouldn't get suspicious. After that I wrote a letter to Kit and one to Mum, ripping the pages out and putting them in the same envelope to post.

In Arithmetic, Sister Agnes moved onto teaching us algebra, while Sister Ambrose was excited about showing us her new pull-down map of the world with all the countries of the Empire coloured in pink.

'The first Empire Games were held last year in Ontario, Canada, and Australia won three gold medals for rowing and swimming. The Olympic Games are being held next year in Los Angeles,' Sister Ambrose said proudly, pointing to each city and country as she named them. 'We should be able to listen to some of the Olympic events on the wireless next year. What do you think about that?'

'What wireless, Sister?' I asked. I really missed listening to the wireless and had thought that there wasn't one at the Farm.

'Henry's been waiting for a part to fix it. It broke a few months ago – all you can hear is crackling.'

Talking about the wireless made me feel homesick. I missed sitting around our AWA wireless with the rest of the family, listening to the cricket, the races, our favourite music and serials, and even the news.

BAD LUCK
CHAPTER 34

Lance left the Farm on the same day that a new boy arrived. I didn't bother saying goodbye or swapping addresses with him. The new boy, Nick, was born in Greece and can't speak English very well but he knows almost as much about farming as Henry. Since Nick arrived, two calves and eleven lambs have been born, including three sets of twins.

After two failed attempts to drive the truck down the road through the mud, Henry finally managed to pick up the bull to mate with some of our cows, just the ones whose milk supply was getting a bit low. Henry's not only a farmer, driver and school caretaker – he's a jack-of-all-trades who can do anything he sets his mind to, and the Three Sisters depend on him.

After picking up a new part for the wireless, Henry fixed it, good as new. Sister Ambrose carried the wireless into the classroom like she was making an offering to the Lord. She plugged it into the generator that sits outside on the verandah and then turned it on so we could listen to the Melbourne Cup. Phar Lap won last year and we all waited impatiently for the champion colt to do it again.

'And they're off in the 1931 Melbourne Cup!' It was hard to understand what the race caller was saying most of the time – he was speaking quickly and there was lots of static. As the horses turned into the straight, running towards the finish line, Phar Lap wasn't mentioned.

'Where's Phar Lap?' I asked in disbelief.

There was more static then the race caller announced, loud and clear. 'And Phar Lap finishes eighth.' I was too shocked to say anything – I'd wanted Phar Lap to win so badly.

It cheered me up a little, though, to think of the money my parents must've won with the hot favourite losing.

Two days later, we were back in the classroom, listening to the wireless, and it wasn't even raining. It was the first day of the Sheffield Shield match between New South Wales and Queensland. Sister Ambrose loves cricket and, like me, she's one of Don Bradman's biggest fans. The radio announcer took us through the highlights of the match, play by play. When Don Bradman walked out to bat, the big crowd at the Gabba stood up and cheered.

Wendell Bill had just been caught behind for a golden duck, and it was up to Bradman to put the first score on the board for New South Wales. He was facing Eddie Gilbert, an Aboriginal bowler from Queensland, and the fastest in the state.

'Bradman easily blocked the second delivery from Gilbert,' the radio announcer reported.

We waited expectantly for the next ball.

'The delivery was short and clipped the top of Bradman's cap, making him lose his balance and fall backwards.'

Sister Ambrose gasped but nobody said a word. I was sitting on the edge of my seat.

'The fourth ball flew over Bradman's head, straight to the keeper.'

I breathed a sigh of relief and edged closer to the wireless.

'The fifth delivery from Gilbert was so fast that it knocked the bat right out of Bradman's hands.'

Everyone gasped – we couldn't believe what we were hearing. *How fast must that ball have been going?* I thought.

There was only one more delivery left in the over. You could've cut the tension in our classroom with a knife.

'He's out!' said the radio announcer. 'Bradman tried to hook the sixth delivery from Gilbert and was caught by Waterman, the wicket keeper. He's out for a duck!'

'He can't be!' I shouted, jumping to my feet. That was the second time in less than a year, I couldn't believe it! Sister Ambrose started to cry and I almost did too. Our hero was out for a duck! It was a shock for me to realise that even the great Don Bradman has bad days and this one was worse than most. 'He'll come good,' I said, with all the confidence in the world. 'Just you wait and see.'

I got a letter back from Mum the following week and I read it while sitting under one of the flame trees eating my lunch.

Dear Joe,

I was very pleased to get your letter and to find you are well and that you are learning lots of new things. I wish I could be there to see you milking the cows and chopping wood. I'm so proud of you. The Sisters sound very kind and I'm sure that you have been learning a lot from them.

We have all been well except for your father. He had a couple of turns recently but is a lot better. The doctor says it's his heart, and told him to take it easy and stay off the grog, which as you know is easier said than done. As soon as he was well enough, he went to see the Monsignor at St Bart's. It didn't go very well. I'm sorry, Joe, but you won't be going back there next year. If your report from St Mary's Farm School is good, you won't have to go back there either.

I can't wait to see you again – you're probably as tall as your father by now. It will be a very special Christmas this year with all of us together once again.

Your loving mother
PS We're all praying that Phar Lap loses the Melbourne Cup.

'You little beauty! Good onya Dad!' I said, looking up at the flame trees and the bright-red buds about to burst into flower. I wish I could've been a fly on the wall when Dad went to see the Monsignor. I couldn't wait to go home and find out what happened.

There was a lot of work to do on the farm before we could go home for Christmas: piles of wood to be chopped, split and stacked; charcoal to be dug up and new pits made; spring and summer veggies to be picked, and new seeds sown and seedlings planted; and all the stock checked and fire breaks made.

It was hard trying to keep the water up to the veggies and fruit trees. It had been a hot spring and early summer, with bushfires already raging and causing havoc in some parts of the country.

A gang of labourers was coming to help Henry on the farm for the six weeks we'd be away. Even the Three Sisters were going on holidays up to Manly beach in Sydney. Half their luck!

On our second-last day at the Farm, we had to scrub every inch of the cabins and shower shed, inside and out. I dragged my mattress outside to beat all the bed bugs out that had been biting me for the past six months.

We all pitched in to clean out the barn and stables, replace the hay, and then spread the old hay and manure on the veggie garden and around the fruit trees.

After lunch, Pete, Charlie and I moved all the desks out of the classroom. I took down Sister Ambrose's charts and maps then washed the blackboard while Charlie and Pete mopped and scrubbed the floor.

Every couple of minutes, I'd call out in my best Irish accent: 'Put a bit more elbow grease into it, boys,' trying to sound just like Sister Agnes.

When Pete threw his scrubbing brush at me, the water fight was on. We tossed wet rags at each other, and then when I was about to throw my bucket of water at them, I slipped on the wet floor and went sliding into the wall.

'I thought you boys were supposed to be washing the floor, not playing on it!' Sister Agnes said, hitting her cane on the door frame. 'I want this mess cleaned up now!'

GOING HOME

CHAPTER 35

On our last morning, I could feel the excitement in the air. We got extra-large bowls of porridge, but no bread this time. Instead, Mrs Lucas baked Anzac biscuits for all of us to take home on the train.

Just for fun, I tried on my St Bart's uniform that I'd worn to the Farm six months ago: grey shorts, blue shirt, blazer, striped tie and matching socks, and black leather shoes. My shorts, shirt, blazer and socks were all too small and I had to squash my toes to fit into my shoes. I'd well and truly outgrown my St Bart's uniform. I wore the clean shirt, trousers and shoes that Sister Agnes gave me instead, and then threw my uniform into the incinerator.

'Ya looked stupid in it anyway,' Pete said, looking over my shoulder at the burning uniform.

As I watched the school crest on my blazer engulfed by flames, I thought about St Bart's – my best friends, Mac and Teddy, and the good times we had there. It wasn't all bad. There was only one bad egg – Brother Felix – and if it wasn't for him I'd probably still be at St Bart's. But then I wouldn't have met Pete and Charlie and gone Racing the Moon. 'We've all got to learn to take the good with the bad.' That's what Mum says, and I think she might be right.

'Ya gunna stay here all day an' watch that fire?' Pete asked.

'I just want to make sure it all burns.'

'Ya hate it that much?'

'Not anymore.'

Before getting into the back of the truck for the trip to the railway station, we said prayers with the Three Sisters and sang, 'O Come All Ye Faithful'. Sister Ambrose's and Sister Cornelius's voices hadn't improved at all over the last six months – if anything, they were worse. As we lined up, waiting our turn to get onto the truck, Sister Agnes gave each of us two shillings and shook our hands. Then we shook hands with Sister Ambrose and Sister Cornelius, and climbed into the back of the truck. We didn't all fit, so some of the boys went in the horse-drawn cart with Nick volunteering to drive. Mrs Lucas had to come as well to bring the horses and cart back while Henry drove the truck.

Sister Agnes cleared her throat to speak. 'Father Brian sends his apologies – he's terribly sorry he isn't here to say goodbye to all of you. He has a baptism to do in Dapto this morning. We wish you all a happy and holy Christmas, and unfortunately we'll be seeing some of you back here again next year.' None of us knew who was coming back – it all depended on the reports that Sister Agnes had already posted to our parents and old schools. In some ways I wanted to come back – the Farm was starting to grow on me. But it wasn't home.

At Yallah railway station, we said our goodbyes to Henry and Mrs Lucas, and then split into two groups: those catching the train south to Bomaderry, including Charlie, and the mob heading north to Sydney, including Pete and me. Nick was the only exception – he pocketed his two shillings and headed up the road to hitch a ride. Said he was heading out west to become a shearer. *Good luck to him*, I thought.

We had the last train carriage to ourselves, because neither of the two people waiting on the platform got in with us, and a woman who had been sitting down, got up and walked through to the next carriage. We must've had 'reformatory' written all over us.

I sat opposite Pete and we looked out the window as the train rattled and rolled through farmlands and past the big lake, stopping first at Dapto then heading towards the ocean and the smoking chimney stacks of Port Kembla.

'Do ya think ya'll be goin' back to the Farm next year?' Pete asked.

'Dunno. What about you?'

'Not sure what I'll be doin' now me stepdad's in gaol. If me report's good enough, I'll probably hafta work to bring in money for Mum an' me two little sisters. Might look around an' find an apprenticeship somewhere, maybe at the steelworks.'

'Henry said they're laying people off there. If you can't find a job, we could go into business together.'

'What kind o' business?'

'Selling eggs and newspapers; a bit of gambling, bookmaking – that kind of thing.'

'What 'bout ya mate, Harry?'

'He's given it all up to help his dad with odd jobs around the neighbourhood.'

'I might be interested then.'

As the train pulled out of Wollongong station, I could see the lighthouse on the headland and fishing boats in the harbour. I kept looking for ships out at sea, and by the time we got to the high bridge over Stanwell Creek, I'd counted three.

'You ever been in a ship, Pete?'

'Nuh. How 'bout you?'

'No, but a friend of mine has. Mac sailed to Batavia in the Dutch East Indies, and then flew to Amsterdam. They mustn't be part of the British Empire because neither of them were coloured pink on Sister Ambrose's new map.' As the train entered a long dark tunnel, I closed the window before the smoke and fumes could come in.

'Was ya dad in the war?' Pete asked.

'On the Western Front with Uncle George, but they never talk about it.'

'Me real dad could've been in the same battalion as ya dad an' uncle. He got killed in the war before I was born. I wanna go to war an' fight one day, just like Dad did.'

'Who would you fight?' I asked.

'The enemy.'

Fair enough, I thought.

'Would ya come with me, Joe?'

'Going to war isn't like Racing the Moon, Pete. It's not something you do on a whim. I think you're jumping the gun, getting a bit ahead of yourself, mate. There's not even a war for us to fight in. We could start off small, you know, selling eggs and newspapers, a bit of gambling and bookmaking on the side, that kind of thing. You ever build a billycart?'

'That's kids' stuff!'

Looking out the window at the grimy factories and run-down shops along the railway line, I wasn't keen to be going back to the city. But when I thought about seeing my family again, I started to get excited. As the train pulled into Central Station, Pete and I grabbed our cases and stood in the doorway, waiting for the train to slow down just enough to jump off, like I always do.

'Joe!'

I could hear Kit but couldn't see him. Then I saw a skinny arm waving and a blond head bobbing up and down in the middle of the crowd waiting on the platform. Mum and Noni were there too, dressed in their Sunday best. Dad was with them, looking thinner than he did six months ago.

'Can you see your mum and little sisters anywhere?' I asked Pete.

'They're always runnin' late.'

'I can wait with you if you like?'

'I'll be right. Ya family are all waitin'. I'll see ya later, mate!'

'You bet!' Pete and I did our special handshake, finishing with a bear hug. As soon as I let go, Kit spear-tackled me, knocking me over.

'Get up, both of you!' Mum said, looking embarrassed. When I got to my feet, I lifted Mum up, swinging her around in the middle of the platform.

'Put me down!' she said, laughing.

Noni was looking the other way, ignoring me. She looked very grown-up, wearing a fancy hat and carrying a handbag just like Mum's. 'G'day Noni,' I said. 'You didn't have to get all dressed up for me.'

'I didn't.'

'She's going to the pictures with Fred,' Kit said.

'Who's this Fred character?' I asked, winking at Kit.

'A friend,' Noni said, pulling on a pair of white gloves.

'You've been behaving yourself for a change, I hear?' Dad said, patting me on the back. It almost felt friendly.

'Did you get my report?'

'We sure did,' Dad replied.

'We're proud of you, Joe,' Mum said, wiping her eyes with a hanky. When I looked around for Pete, he was gone. Mum took hold of my hand: 'Sister Agnes is very pleased with the progress you've made, so that means you can stay home and go to school here next year.'

'Not to St Bart's!' I snapped.

'You won't be going back there, don't worry about that,' Dad said, clenching and unclenching his fists.

'You're not leaving me ever again, I won't let you,' Kit said, trying to put me in a headlock.

'I'll race you to the tram,' I said, pushing him off me and getting a head start. Looking over my shoulder, I called out: 'I bags the bed under the window!' then started running for my life through Central Station to catch the tram back home to Glebe.

AUTHOR'S NOTE

I was inspired to write this book by stories my uncle told me about growing up in Sydney during the 1930s. *Racing the Moon* is set in 1931 and follows a year in the life of Joe Riley. I've tried to convey what it was like to be a boy, living and going to school during the Depression. I want the reader to be right there with Joe – seeing, feeling and experiencing everything that he does, to get a personal understanding of what it was like growing up at this difficult time in Australia's history.

Very few families had a car or even a telephone back then. Most people in Sydney caught trams or trains to get around, or else walked. Aviators like Charles Kingsford Smith were flying around in small planes and commercial flights were just starting out. Ships were used to transport goods and people around the world, but only the wealthy could afford to travel. Computers weren't invented, there was no television and the film industry was just starting up. Apart from listening to the wireless or gramophone records, people had to make their own entertainment at home.

Most people consider the American stock market crash in 1929 to be the start of the Great Depression. As prices for our primary produce (mainly wool and wheat) collapsed and overseas loan funds dried up, businesses closed, the government cut back on services and staff, and many people lost their jobs. The Bank of England advised our government on what needed to be done for Australia to be able to pay back its loans. In 1931, the government cut the basic wage by ten per cent, increased taxes and slashed spending. By 1932, around thirty per cent of Australian workers were unemployed, while many of those with jobs had to accept pay cuts or part-time employment.

The government provided some relief to the unemployed through the dole or sustenance (known as 'susso'), but it was barely enough to survive on, and consisted mostly of food vouchers and coupons that could be exchanged for basic food items like bread, butter and meat. Soup kitchens and bread lines were organised by churches and other charities to help the destitute. There was no rent support provided by the government so a lot of people were forced to leave their homes and live in shanty towns or on the streets and in parks. Many people had to be creative to make ends meet during the Depression – just like Joe and his family.

ACKNOWLEDGEMENTS

With many thanks to Lyn Tranter, Anna McFarlane and Rachael Donovan for their expert advice, ongoing support, enthusiasm for the book, and belief in me. Thanks also to Kate Goldsworthy and Nan McNab for their wonderful editing and proof-reading skills, and to Sue Hines and Irina Dunn who were enthusiastic about the book from the very beginning.

A big thank you and much love to my family and friends who read *Racing the Moon* during its adolescence and provided welcome feedback and encouragement: to Luke (my husband, soulmate and number one reader and supporter), Ben, Lindsey, Sylvia, Geoff, Wendy, Carol and Jonathan, and to Becky, Lee, Toby and Holly for their support as well.

With appreciation to David Wells and the Bradman Foundation for their authoritative information on Sir Donald Bradman and Eddie Gilbert.

With love and gratitude to Ron and Ray Morgan (my father and uncle), a couple of lads who grew up in the Depression.

And finally thank you to all my readers! To find out more about me, visit michellejmorgan.com.au. You can also find me on Facebook or Twitter @mjmorganwriter.